GREAT BRITISH HORROR X

SOMETHING PECULIAR

Great British Horror X
Something Peculiar

Edited by
Steve J Shaw

BLACK
SHUCK
BOOKS

First published in Great Britain in 2025 by
Black Shuck Books
Kent, UK

Set in Caslon by WHITEspace
www.white-space.uk

Cover design from
'The Origins', by Odilon Redon,
courtesy of The Museum of Fine Arts, Boston
Cover and interior layout © WHITEspace, 2024

978-1-917173-08-7

In memory of David Lynch

Introduction

I honestly never thought I'd be writing this.

I first started approaching authors about the *Great British Horror* series in 2015; I was an inexperienced editor with just two anthologies to my name, and an even more inexperienced publisher, having only released one book through Black Shuck. To my surprise, the response was very positive, and eleven established authors entrusted their work to a complete unknown. Ten years later, 111 writers have featured across ten volumes, three of those volumes have been nominated for British Fantasy Awards, and stories have been nominated for both British Fantasy and Bram Stoker Awards. I have been delighted by the ongoing response to this series – but as the saying goes, all good things…

This will be the final volume under the *Great British Horror* title. The series will continue, but with a few changes. Starting next year, the series title will be changing to *Something Peculiar*, reflecting the series' move from solely horror writing into a wider range of weird fiction, as well as broadening its horizons away from exclusively UK-set stories. One thing that won't be changing, however, is the quality of the writing. Volume XI will once again feature a mix of established and upcoming authors at the top of their game, telling peculiar tales of this sceptered isle, and beyond…

I want to take this opportunity to extend my thanks to a few people. Firstly, the aforementioned authors, who have taken this series from a one-off passion project to an ongoing annual anthology:

C C Adams, Guy Adams, G V Anderson, Tiffani Angus, Allen Ashley, Jenn Ashworth, Simon Avery, Stephen Bacon, Jasper Bark, Lena Beasley-Silverwood, A K Benedict, Simon Bestwick, Holly Blades, Charlotte Bond, James Brogden, Sarah Brooks, Georgina Bruce, Gary Budden, M R Carey, Simon Clark, Ray Cluley, Dan Coxon, Kath Deakin, Malcolm Devlin, Steven J Dines, Steve Duffy, Jan Edwards, Kayleigh Marie Edwards, Brian Evenson, James Everington, Paul M Feeney, Gemma Files, Paul Finch, Andrew Freudenberg, Gary Fry, Stephen Gallagher, Cate Gardner, Emma J Gibbon, Helen Grant, Muriel Gray, Rich Hawkins, Grady Hendrix, Sean Hogan, Verity Holloway, Carly Holmes, Andrew Hook, Stewart Hotston, Andy Humphrey, Maxim Jakubowski, Timothy J Jarvis, Carole Johnstone, Penny Jones, Paul Kane, Ida Keogh, Shona Kinsella, Rachel Knightley, John Langan, Stephen Laws, Tim Lebbon, V H Leslie, Alison Littlewood, Sarah Lotz, Johnny Mains, Tim Major, Laura Mauro, Maura McHugh, Lucie McKnight Hardy, Gary McMahon, Paul Meloy, Adam Millard, Alexander Milner, David Moody, Alison Moore, Mark Morris, Lisa Morton, Linda Nagle, Thana Niveau, Jonathan Oliver, Reggie Oliver, Marie O'Regan, Rosalie Parker, Kit Power, John Llewellyn Probert, Rosanne Rabinowitz, Nicholas Royle, Lynda E Rucker, Priya Sharma, Robert Shearman, Jonathan Sims, Angela Slatter, Phil Sloman, Guy N Smith, Michaael Marshall Smith, Teika Marija Smits, Ashley Stokes, Anna Taborska, Steve Toase, Lisa Tuttle, Simon Kurt Unsworth, Stephen Volk, Damien Angelica Walters, Catriona Ward, Danie Ware, Ren Warom, Kelly White, Aliya Whiteley, Barbie Wilde, Ally Wilkes, Conrad Williams, Marian Womack and C A Yates.

And thank you to everyone who has read, reviewed and discussed the series so far. Hopefully we can continue to enjoy new stories together for many years to come.

Steve J Shaw
September 2025

Something Peculiar

from

Holly Blades

Forest

"…these dark emotions…"

IT HAS been a long and fruitful autumn leading into an unseasonably warm early winter. The killing frost has not yet been, and the world seems in a stasis of clinging to what life remains in the fall, and succumbing to the approaching death of the hoar.

It's dusk when I see two men enter the clearing, and I am rigid. All around me, the leaves sound as loud as waves on a beach. The evergreen cypress and pine, and those other crisp brown remnants that persist, refusing to abandon their branches. I want to shush them, I want to hear what these two men – men who don't belong here – are saying.

Why they have come to my sanctuary.

They speak in low voices. The robins and starlings are still singing too loudly in the fading winter sun, boughs are creaking like heavy doors, and somewhere in the distance I can hear a fox scream. The low and quiet rumble of their conversation melts into the sound of the woodland and I'm increasingly frustrated that I can't fully understand them.

…looks good…

Deserted…

They're gesturing, left and right, tipping over centuries old forest debris with the scuffed toes of their leather boots. One crouches down and peers into the largest of the fallen trunks – I think it was an old diseased oak but it has been there so long I forget. He pokes a gloved hand cautiously into the dark interior and I feel a small tickle of joy when he falls back, uttering a disgusted shriek and batting small spiders from his tunic.

Shhhh

...beasts...

The younger man – still hopping from foot to foot, scraping now imaginary cobwebs from his sleeves – is taller than his companion. Dark curly hair and ruddy skin. His hands seem as large as spades and his shoulders as broad as an ox. He looks as though he works in the sun. The other man is small and old. From my vantage point, as he stands with his back to me, I can just see the top of his head. The skin of his scalp visible through his wispy white hair. He is almost too pink; it feels like an indecent colour for an adult to be. He looks like an elderly baby, all angry newborn skin and hunched bony shoulders clashing with the snow-whiteness of his hair and the liver spots on his clawed and ungloved hands. He turns in my direction and his watery blue eyes dart around the clearing. I feel increasingly uneasy. His is not a good soul.

It's not as though I'm near to the men. They won't see me watching them. But it is still so rare for people to come here. Children pass through sometimes – they don't raise concern, their laughter might pierce the quiet as they brandish small branches as swords – but it is the adults that give me pause. It has been my experience that adults rarely come here with admirable or noble purpose. That in itself is enough to send shivers of disquiet through me.

Hurry...

...no rush...perfect..

I can see the entire clearing from up here. I can see the swan's neck moss covering the shaded corner of the glade, the corner that gives slightly as the older man steps back, treading on the soft green carpet that covers rotten floorboards. I can see the lichen – oakmoss, lungwort, trumpet – growing from the craggy bark, both living and dead. But nothing really dies here. I think that's why I love it so much, why I feel so protective of this space, this clearing, this whole forest. What dies becomes life. The rich yellow sulphur shelf spreads like coral. and stinkhorns sprout from the crevices between the fallen wood. A long time ago, decades maybe, the old beech tree in the southern corner of the clearing was home to a mating swift pair. They returned every year and I watched them raise their family. The beech was struck by lightning years ago. Now it plays occasional home to an aggressive tawny owl. Death will find life.

The men are still investigating. Examining the trees, lifting fallen branches and brushing leaf piles aside.

...*fast*...

...*shall we go*...

At one point they come near enough that I think they will see me. But they don't. Finally they mutter a few words to each other and retreat the way they came.

The clearing suddenly seems silent again, like the noise of the forest crescendoed to submerge their activity, to drown the tall man's gruff rumblings and the old man's nasal whine, and now it can relax again.

It is a short-lived peace.

Life seems to continue as normal. I exist. I breathe. I drink. I eat. Sometimes I think I might even sleep when the nights seem shorter than they should be. I see the sun rise and set, but when the sunrise and its accompanying birdsong appear to roll around when night has only just reached its deepest inky blackness... that's when I can believe I have slept. Maybe the darkest hour truly is just before dawn.

On the fourth rising of the sun since the men first appeared, they return. Once again I am frozen in place, suppressing my urge to move. And once again the rising cacophony of nature seems to shake the earth like the forest is protesting their presence. But I am silently trembling and I don't know whether it is the wind, the anticipation, or my own fear.

Their clothes are stained, with mud or with blood I can't tell. Thick brown patches on their breeches and tunics. There is a sense of urgency about the intruders, as I now think of them, on this occasion. The younger one carries a clanging hessian sack of some weight. The noise of its contents adding to the roar of nature. The old man is stumbling in his excitement, tripping over his dirty boots and flailing his thin arms. He gestures with both of his too-pink hands towards the spider-filled tree trunk. The younger man pauses, recoils even, and they exchange more grimaced words lost under the din of the forest.

…laugh…again…

…scared…child…

The old man's pale hands grab at the sack but the ruddy faced youth is nimble and evades his crooked, knotted fingers. He seems to brace himself before shouldering the smaller wizened figure out of his way. The sack is unceremoniously pushed deep into the trunk. I wish I could see the contents from this vantage point but the sack appears to be tied tightly, and the hanging lichen restricts my view of its resting place.

…few weeks…

…clear…safe…

The two figures loiter, as though neither wants to be the first to leave the clearing, eyes darting between each other and the hidden sack. Finally the old man bats the younger man lightly with his fingertips, shooing him away from the tree trunk, out of my line of sight, and towards the outer edges of the forest.

❖

It's summer now. The sunshine dapples the mossy ground, and while the corners of the forest may still be dark and dank, there is a feeling of lightness in the air, like a weight has been lifted, like life is in full swing. I've watched the woodland creatures come and go. Bats soar between boles, picking insects out of the air before returning to their roosts. There are tiny snuffling hedgehogs, minds lost to anything but the damp ground beneath their feet. I've seen grey squirrels darting between the now verdant canopy of leaves, jerking to a halt to sniff the air or cast enquiring eyes over the branches surrounding them, like they have heard something I haven't, or have remembered something they had previously forgotten. Maybe they have. The activity of life is evident all around from the woodlice to the owls, the earthworms to the foxes, but as the dead leaves feed their living kin, as the owl roosts in the lightning tree, that life will also find death.

And so the men return again. Cautiously, as before, glancing back into the depth of the woods. Back along the rarely-travelled path they have walked too many times already. For once, the clearing is silent. There is a feeling of suspense hanging in the warm air, and I wait.

…still there…

Go look…

The older man crouches down, towards where the sodden and mildewed corner of their sack is still just visible within the old log. He wipes his brow and his wispy hair stands on end, then he reaches his small uncanny fingers into the log and grasps the wet burlap. He doesn't notice the other man approaching him from behind with a heavy branch in his hands. His wide blue eyes look startled for a moment, and I know he is questioning what has just happened, before all questions cease and his world – and with it, his loves, his hates, his joys, his pains – is extinguished.

One hit would have been enough, but the younger man keeps going. I wonder what must have happened between them for the rage to be so intense, yet as the old man falls, he pulls the sack from its hiding place and something silver and lustrous falls into the dappled sunshine. It must be valuable. The younger man pushes the crumpled body on its back and looks down at what used to be its face. A face that had held a tight angry mouth and sunken pale eyes, but a face all the same.

I think he is going to say something, more scattered words that I can hardly make out, but instead he reaches down, looping an arm under each shoulder. He pulls the deadweight over towards me, presumably away from the entrance to the clearing, and I am motionless, whether with fear or expectation I am not sure. He doesn't notice me, but I can now see the smears of the old man's thoughts over the front of his shirt. I can see every speck of blood, of bone, of matter, in the place where the corpse's pathetic white hair used to be. I remain transfixed as the young man spits once on the pile of rags and skin, collects his spoils and silently leaves, whistling to himself as he does so.

The old man is close enough that he could touch me if he still had the ability to move those paper-thin arms. Instead, they lie useless at his sides, the sleeves rucked up to his shoulders, the pinched, sagging skin around his joints lying like the jelly ear on the elder bush. His legs have folded beneath him and that, combined with the odd delicateness of the patches of his unblemished skin, makes him appear like a sleeping child – if it weren't for the chaos that used to be his head. A head that saw, that tasted, that kissed. A brain that thought, that felt, that dreamed, that schemed. And that hated. Something about the two intruders, their disrespect for my refuge, their obvious dislike of each other, tells me that hate was one of the few feelings they held in common. I've never hated anything but I know it is an emotion a lot of mankind feels. The younger man hated this poor bundle of bloody clothing enough to end his long life.

Whilst I don't want to look, more out of respect for what was once a human being than any kind of repulsion, I can't help it. I can't tear myself away. It's been a long time since I last saw a dead body, and that little slip of a thing that died peacefully in her sleep was fascinating in a different way. She exuded life, and kindness, and an affinity to nature. She may have been at home in this shelter, but her tiny frame could not take the winter cold, even if she did feel safer sleeping amongst the trees and the creatures of the forest than wherever there was a bed waiting for her.

Looking at the scene below, the scattered matter and quickly-darkening red telling the story of a brutal execution, it's hard to believe that any of that blood could remain in the old man's small frame. But, as that which is left in his body – that which hasn't either plastered the ground by the fallen tree trunk, smeared across the moss and bark, or stained his crony's clothing – as that enduring blood begins to pool in his stationary limbs, the awful pinkness begins to fade, replaced by a pallid grey that actually seems to make the unmutilated parts of his body look more human. And soon the summer showers will come and the brown stains will wash away. I feel safe in the knowledge that order, the order of the forest, will return.

The old man begins to decompose much quicker than the girl did. The clearing may only be spotted with sunlight, but it is summer here and there is no denying that. Some of the creatures love the heat. I've seen foxes playing in the clearing during the long summer evenings, only casting occasional glances to the pile of rags in the corner. They drop by the body, paws out and brushes raised, before dashing and rolling together around the greenery. If you observe them long enough, their games seem to make sense, to have rules. It's one of my favourite things to watch. The other is the bees. There aren't a lot of flowers in this glade but in the spring and summer the bees cover the lavender that grows in the sunnier patches. I love to watch them work.

It has been days and he is bloated now. The insects are arriving, and the constant drone of the blowflies is unnerving, but I appreciate their service. Soon he will begin to liquefy and release himself to the earth. I saw it happen to a sick badger once. Whilst the viscera was eaten, scavenged or absorbed, the fur remained for many years, tufts here and there, a reminder of his previous existence. The old man's fine white hair won't last that long, I'm sure.

Some lucky blue tit is going to have a soft nest come the new year. Once again, from death comes life.

I think of that poor young waif again. So thin, so pale. She was different – the snow preserved her 'til the spring came again, then it didn't take long for her tiny body to succumb to the heat amongst the bluebells and snowdrops. It felt like the creatures respected her. Like the crumple of angles that were her remains were hallowed. Her bones are still down there, protected, hidden among the undergrowth. I wonder if any of her kin miss her?

Maybe she really was hallowed – a fae or a crone. There seemed to be changes within the forest after she appeared. Changes to the birdsong, changes to the scavengers, changes to the very atoms of the clearing. Changes to myself. I had stood witness for so many years but then I started to alter.

To change, and more importantly, to learn.

I was incredibly old when I began to learn – to question, to name and to think. I don't communicate in your usual way as I have no mouth, and I have no lungs, but the power of thought was a revelation. Those things I had done purely because nature had intended, I now had words for.

It was around my hundredth winter when that poor girl crawled up beside me and fell asleep for the last time. I had been there, solid, silent, observing as I always am, but as she broke down and became one with the loamy earth at my base, there was a change. I felt something. Not the sharp feeling of young boys driving knives into me to carve their symbols and emblems, but a heaviness in my core. A weight that made the forest, even in late spring, feel drab and grey.

As I soaked up more lingering nutrients from the ground, I learned the feeling was sadness. The girl was sad to her very soul, a soul she had feared for. A soul that had been persecuted for her affinity with nature. She taught me the names of the creatures that played in the forest, the names of the trees that sheltered them. When there was nothing but her bones remaining, I felt connected to her. But connected to more than just her. I felt pathways of information bleeding into me from miles around, seeping into my nascent consciousness. I joined kin several yards away, they joined kin several yards away and suddenly I was overwhelmed with knowledge, from those like me who stood sentry over *hundreds* of souls. Greying stone teeth crumbling under watchful yews and wildflower thickets. I knew everything they had once known because of her.

I wonder if I am harbouring her, keeping her soul safe until she can reclaim it – it would be safer with me than any of her deities. I wonder if I harbour all the souls I have absorbed?

The old man is no different to those decomposing on the edge of the forest, behind the lychgate. He is just one more angry, vain creature, brought down by his assumption that he is not a fool, and by his inherent foolishness. He has given me new memories, more four letter words for emotions and activities that I cannot comprehend, but other than that, he has taught me nothing. It is true his proximity must amplify some of his baser emotions because profuse feelings of futility are the main thing I take away from him – that humans are weak, and therefore dangerous. This is interesting knowledge. This is why he allowed his greed to overtake him, and why he was finally able to be eliminated by someone he never trusted to begin with. These are all emotions I am already familiar with, but were held within him in such mass that it makes me uncomfortable to feel them now. Humans can be so blind. So scared, so stupid and so very greedy.

I stretch myself out so my branches untwist momentarily, creaking like my late brethren in an ancient hull, and turn my gently rustling leaves to the sun. We will hold this corrupting knowledge, these dark emotions, we will learn from them, and we will use them when we need to, against the unwary whose ancestors have taught us.

Something Peculiar

from

Guy Adams

Holly Blade

Sarah Brook

Emma J. Gibbon

Timothy J. Jarvis

John Langan

Tim Major

Alexander Milner

Mark Morris

Danie Ware

Marian Womack

Cemetery Black

"...fairytales seldom bloom in concrete jungles..."

THE PARANORMAL does not exist. It never has. We create stories to deal with trauma. Sometimes that trauma can be shared and felt collectively within a community, forever evolving through retellings; captured in various mediums to perpetuate – and sometimes profit upon – said trauma.

That *was* my truth.

I boarded the plane from Birmingham Airport. I was meant to be rewarded by a sunset view as I flew north to Glasgow. Instead, the flight was delayed, so I spent that sweltering summer evening in the terminal, watching the sunset over the grey tarmac.

Annoyingly, my connecting flight to the small airport near Campbeltown would have to be replaced by a long, and gravely expensive, taxi ride from Glasgow Airport. Darkness enveloped the world as it does every night. The airport was well lit, but silent, except for intermittent coughing and the sipping of overpriced airport coffee.

Once I was finally in the air, the only friend I had was the blinking red light on the wing, revealing an empty void below as well as above. That constant flicker of life, sandwiched between oblivion.

I had spent my life travelling the world, and it always made me wonder: once humankind had pierced the clouds and found heaven's zenith, had we begun to look toward the stars for meaning? One step closer to God, only to find out we had many flights to go. Our belief in the paranormal operated in the same way – each push to find the next *weird* thing further expanded that boundary of what we thought of as truth.

I digress, because *she* was there. Not *with* me, but there nonetheless. *She* had been since the airport, and far longer before. Reflected in the window, accompanied only by the red flicker; each time a new configuration of scars and decay. A doppelganger of a doppelganger. Because memory is kind, if it is fresh. But it too decays.

Her voice, *her* scent, *her* face. Now a husk. Never again the same. But *she* followed me on every journey, in every reflection.

The moment the plane landed in Glasgow and it was safe to take off my belt I rushed for my bag and made for the front of the plane. Admittedly, it wasn't the most cordial thing to do after an hour's flight, but what with getting to Birmingham Airport two hours early for security, the three-hour delay, and the flight, it had been a while since I had the sweet release of nicotine.

To my surprise, waiting for me in the arrivals lounge was someone holding a sign: *Matlock*.

The woman leant on the railing with a coffee in her free hand, lazily holding the sign. Her blonde hair was tied up in a messy bun; counting the number of empty takeaway cups in the bin beside her, it was clear her once prim figure had fallen to tiredness and no longer cared to keep up appearances.

Her eyes locked on mine, and she waved me over. I awkwardly waved back, as I had never seen her before.

"Taylor Matlock," she said. "I am Dana Lithgow, senior journalist at the Campbeltown Gazette."

A fucking *journalist*. Don't get me wrong, I think journalists are the skid marks of society; however, while I'd expected an expression of pure arrogance and self-importance, instead I saw a face I could only describe as weathered.

"Forgive me," I said, "I wasn't aware of a journalist meeting me."

Dana held her hand out toward my bag and I accepted her support. My arms were tired, and old age was catching up with me. "I was made aware of your delayed trip, and I'm willing to offer my support."

"I don't need a tour guide."

"Less of a tour guide, more of a liaison, and at this point in time, a sofa to sleep on." Her voice was raspy from either a life waiting in cold bushes to get a front-page scoop, or from countless nights nursing a bottle of whiskey. Possibly both.

I raised a brow. I'm not in my prime, but I'm not exactly on death's door either. I have spent many years sleeping in yurts, on floors, and sometimes war zones; she must've known this because no self-respecting person would look at someone pushing sixty and offer them a sofa to sleep on. I was suspicious to say the least.

She took my bag to her car. The crisp early morning air hit me as I lit up a cigarette. The last thing I wanted was to be pounced on by a journalist, but I wasn't going to turn down the free accommodation – I had spent time in worse conditions, but only barely. After my nicotine release, I got into the car.

For a senior journalist, the car wasn't anything to gawp at. A silver Ford Mondeo, with grey interior and a pine car freshener hanging from the rear-view mirror – which I was sure was against the Highway Code, but I kept that to myself. Take That played quietly from the iPod, tempting me to do a tactical roll out of the car at the next red light.

Dana cleared her throat – not an unusual gesture but coming from a journalist had a certain eye-rolling edge to it.

"It's going to be about three hours," she said. "Feel free to get a kip in if you like."

"No thank you," I said, a bit more grumpily than I had hoped. I could feel my eyes drooping, and, despite my best judgement, thought a little conversation would perk me up. That, and *her* reflection was watching. "Local, are you?"

"Glaswegian born and bred," she said. "Though I moved out to Campbeltown a few years ago to get away from the city."

Her accent had evolved into a concoction of well-spoken English with sprinkles of Glaswegian idioms. I too understood the identity-warping lack of a cohesive accent, which leaves one isolated but worldly.

"And your brother is Jason Lithgow, correct?" I had heard his name a few times during my travels. Most journalists were monsters, but Jason had a special place in hell for twisting stories to meet his agenda.

Dana cleared her throat. I suspected a level of disappointment for her kin, especially as she had taken a journalist job in a small town in the arse end of nowhere. She said nothing for the next two hours, which I suppose was a win. I didn't even realise I had fallen asleep; the last images I saw were of *her*.

I awoke on a sofa. It was scratchy, but otherwise comfortable. Dana's living room was simplistic: beige and white, hardly inspirational, but clean at least. She did not have much in the way of decor or knick-knacks, and certainly no self-indulgent paper clippings framed onto the wall to gloat to friends when passing hors d'oeuvres.

I woke early. Call me old if you like, but there's something otherworldly about waking up with the sun, that feeling of the veil restitching itself for another day of reality; that tether of the real, wound up and protected for another day.

I looked outside the window. The town was quaint – for all its quirks – and had a certain 'edge of the world' charm that would inspire writers as much as it would warn off any young adult with dreams of exuberance.

It never attracted me, not even closing in on retirement. The city was bold, loud, and dirty – but that kept the world's mythological demons at bay, and it thrived on insomnia and night owls. Fairytales seldom bloom in concrete jungles, where the true evil is plain to see.

Dana awoke, giving up the need to look professional. She wore a nightgown, her hair in a messy bun.

"Good morning," she said, heading toward the kitchenette. She filled and flicked on the kettle. "Instant good for you?"

"No problem," I said. I survived by stashing as many hotel instant coffee sachets as I could. It's not stealing if I technically paid for it.

She let out a long yawn. "You're not even a little bit curious to know how I found out why you are here?"

"Not especially," I said. "The community's response to the haunting is big enough that it would inevitably reach this town at some point. But now that I mention it, it's a bit odd that my source directed me here instead of the Isle of Arran." I studied her for a moment. The smug self-satisfaction gave away the truth.

"I knew you wouldn't come if a journalist asked," she said, victoriously.

I rolled my eyes. "It would be a waste to go home now."

"Good," she said with a twinkle in her eye. "Take a shower and get changed. We have a ferry to catch to the Isle."

"You don't waste any time."

"Indeed I don't. I have an interview setup with a local near Glenkiln later today. Elderly lady who has had multiple encounters with those affected."

Dana handed me a coffee. I took a long sip before letting out a deflated breath. "And you know what we seek?"

"Sluagh na Marbh – pretty common fae creature in Celtic folklore. Something I, and many other Scots, have known about since we were wee children. Hence why I am the perfect companion for this trip."

I could not deny her local knowledge would be a bonus. In every trip a guide was paramount, especially when it came to language and culture barriers. If only she wasn't a fucking journalist.

After a shower and a change, we departed. Crossing through the picturesque Campbeltown, protected by the bastion that is Davaar Island. The air was crisp, a far cry from the odious stench of the city, so much so that I had to make up for it with a cigarette or two. The ferry was no better, bombarded by sea mist and the summer sun reflecting upon it. More beautiful than my grumpy mind was willing to admit. But that mostly came from seeing *her* in every plane of water. There was no escape.

We arrived at Brodick no later than noon. The sun beat down upon us as we took refuge in a deli for lunch. Dana ordered a lemonade whilst I stuck to coffee. I'd never had a sweet tooth and did not want to start now. Not much later, we took a cab to the outskirts of Glenkiln. The local gave us a weird look when we told him the location.

The cabbie parked up on the country road at the edge of the woods where it was said that the locals were taken – and later returned.

"Are ye sure this is where you wanna be?" said the cabbie in an accent I had trouble with.

"Aye, sir," said Dana with a forced accent, no doubt to not seem like an outsider. "Keep the change."

The cabbie shrugged and took the money before taking off back to Brodick.

Hidden behind an overgrown hedge stood a cottage torn asunder by the elements and age. The walls were wrapped in ivy, the windows plagued by moss and mildew. The door was tattered and the path unkempt. The front garden barely resembled a garden at all, blending in with the wilds surrounding it.

"Wait a second," I said before we got to the door. "Remember to just let the lady tell her story. We're finding the truth here, not exposing her."

Dana turned with a sour expression. She wanted to say something, but an argument outside an old lady's cottage would not be a good look for either of us. She took a deep breath and knocked on the door.

To further her annoyance – and admittedly my own – no one answered.

Dana knocked again.

I looked through the moss-stained window. The panes of glass were cracked and the only thing I could see was *her*, but fragmented. *She* was looking at me with warning in *her* eyes.

"Fuck sake," said Dana, kicking a half-smashed garden gnome off its pedestal. "I was told that a lady lived here. She must exist."

"Not every lead works out," I said, perhaps with a little bit of smugness in my voice.

Dana sat down on a crumbled wall. "I spent months on this one."

"It happens," I said with a shrug. "Doesn't look like anyone has lived here in years."

It was just a little bit rewarding seeing a cocky journalist reach a dead end, but seeing her pinch the bridge of her nose I wasn't sure whether to be condemning or merciful.

"There's plenty more to report on the isle," I said, attempting to be helpful, but ultimately sounding condescending. "Holiday parks, cafés, heritage sites."

Dana stood, clenching her fist. "You speak of my profession with such bile. Don't you also hunt for the truth? Your blog isn't so different from the tabloid."

I scoffed and didn't even try to hide the guffaw that followed.

"I write the truth. Stone cold truth. If it amounts to nothing, I'm not afraid to own that truth – unlike people such as your brother, who use hyperbole and lies to sell a scoop."

Turning red, Dana pointed a finger at me. "That's a lie."

"The constant twisting and bending of the truth to fit in with an agenda – it's all the same. Journalists only ever interrogate victims, plant truths within their head and project their own egos onto them."

Adrenaline coursed through me, and evidently through her too, based on the way she was breathing heavily; clenching her fists, forehead sweaty. She pointed her finger at me again, this time with more vitriol, and went to speak as the door opened.

"I'm sorry," said the old lady at the door. She was wearing a patterned nightgown and wrapped in a knitted technicolour blanket. "My hearing isn't what it used to be. Come in, I'll pop the kettle on."

Hesitantly, we headed inside. The rage quickly subsided as we entered the decrepit house. Wallpaper peeled off, revealing the brick underneath. Paintings hung crookedly, barely recognisable with the amount of staining. She led us into a living room with a cloth-covered sofa. Water dripped from the ceiling into a near-full bucket of grimy water.

I sat, dust billowing out from under me, I looked at Dana, who was as befuddled as I.

My concern was the poor living standards that the community had left her to. Not that we'd spent that much time on the isle, and the locals had seemed nice enough. But I didn't have the full story. I was there to listen and learn.

Dana and I did not utter a word to one another. It was embarrassing enough to be overheard arguing outside; to bicker in the old lady's house would not only be unprofessional, but downright mortifying.

The old lady came back in with a porcelain tray, three cups and saucers, and a pot of tea with a tattered cosy atop it. She placed it on the table. There was a nip in the air, so I looked toward the window; it was open a crack, and the wind billowed upon the thin net curtain.

"Want me to close the window?" I asked.

The old lady shrugged. "If you're a bit nippy, darling. Of course."

I could smell the bergamot. Earl Grey. My favourite. As I closed the window, *she* was staring at me. A version of *her*, anyway. Each reflection its own unique haunting.

I sat back down and was handed a cup. The handle was smaller than my pinkie, so I had to hold it by the brim. It wasn't as hot as I had thought.

"Geraldine," she said, smiling. "Geraldine McFadden. Or Geraldine O'Leary if you want my maiden name."

"Irish?" said Dana. She received a nod in response. Not that you could tell; her accent had been warped by years on the island.

Dana pulled out a recording device alongside a pad and pen. She looked at me expectantly. I tapped my head. The benefit of eidetic memory.

She switched on the recording device. As she ran through the formalities of the date, who was present, and the topic of the recording, I looked around again. There were no family photos, which was odd for an elderly lady who lived alone. I'd at least expected one of her and her husband.

Dana continued: "Geraldine—"

"Call me Gerry," the old lady said with a sweet smile. One that had never left her face. To be that happy, even in these conditions, was more of a mystery than an achievement. So many smiles are worn as masks in the world, but Gerry was different. It was her truth.

"Gerry," Dana returned with a smile. "Is it true that you have been in contact – or talked to someone in contact – with a Sluagh?"

I winced. I hadn't expected much from a journalist, but to start off like this was unacceptable. Dana invited me to contribute, as though I were a passenger to her greatness.

"Perhaps," I said, arms wide and welcoming, "you can start by telling us what you experienced."

Gerry took a sip of tea. "Over the years, being so close to the forest, I have heard noises—"

"Wails, screams, and such?" said Dana.

"Yes," said Gerry. "Strange noises. I've had folks knock on my door, in the middle of the night, sweating and half-dressed, crazed and covered in dirt—"

"The most recent were Abbie Crawford, Daniel Listerman, and Godric McUlster, correct?"

"Yes, sweetie."

I side eyed Dana, but she was focused on her notepad, writing furiously.

Gerry took another sip of tea, clearing her throat before continuing. "They said they were taken by the Sluagh – know what that is, dear?"

"Why don't you tell us—" I began.

"Sluagh are spirits," said Dana. "Or fae folk. They come in the form of birds, or clouds, or hanging gaunt people. Spirits of death that battle an endless war over the isles of Scotland and Ireland."

My jaw clenched. Just as I assumed. Journalism at its finest.

"Correct again, sweetie," said Gerry. "Well, these young folk were waking up in a cemetery of all things – in the middle of the forest!"

"Interesting," I said. "Tell me more, in your words."

"They all said the same thing: that they woke up in a cemetery made of black gravestones, a black iron fence, and surrounded by a line of black salt."

"Each said the exact same?" I said.

"Indeed."

I squinted.

Dana cleared her throat. "Was there any significance to this graveyard – any names?"

"Yes, sweetie. They each said that they saw their own names."

"And they said where the graveyard is?"

"Well, that's the funny thing," said Gerry. "When any of them tried to return, the graveyard was gone."

Dana tapped her pen on the notepad. "And when did this happen – Halloween, or, well, I mean Samhain?"

Gerry nodded.

"So," I said. "Each victim of the Sluagh went out alone during Samhain and were attacked, but not killed, by the Sluagh?"

"Not every fae tries to kill you," said Dana with a snorted laugh.

"Indeed not," said Gerry. "They all *woke up* on Samhain. Some said they went out during the summer moon, others during winter. Some were gone for months before waking back up again."

There was a triumph to that voice that I couldn't shake off. There wasn't much to the story, and I feared there wouldn't be much more. I wanted to know more about her interpretation of the Sluagh, but every time I tried, Dana answered and was met with an agreeing response. We said our goodbyes after an hour of talking. I didn't even touch my tea.

We walked out in the baking sun, awaiting the cab. We did not speak the whole journey, other than the words "to the library" to the cabbie. He dropped us off and I went straight for the records.

Dana sighed, then walked up to me as I sat, trawling through old newspapers. "That felt a bit off, didn't it?"

I nodded. "That's because she doesn't exist."

All I got in return was a stare of confusion as she sat down next to me. "What do you mean?" she said, in a hushed tone.

"Gerry. The old lady we met at the cottage. She didn't exist. Or at least, hasn't for a decade."

"Seriously, you have to start making some sense," said Dana with a chuckle.

I handed her an obituary from eight years previously. *Geraldine McFadden. Deceased at the age of 96. Natural causes.*

"I, erm, I," said Dana scanning the text. "The fuck? The actual fuck?"

"Trauma," I said.

"*What?*"

"Shared trauma. What we experienced was shared trauma in audio-visual form."

"And how in the fuck did you figure that out?"

"You."

She scoffed. "Me?"

"Well, your inability to not be a narcissistic journalist. All you did during the conversation was perpetuate the story, feeding it. You never let Gerry – or what you thought was Gerry – answer any questions with intent. They just repeated what you said and sometimes added in what is already public knowledge."

I handed her another newspaper clipping. Daniel Listerman: said to have been 'kidnapped' by a Sluagh in 1991. It was said he'd fallen into a bout of depression following the death of his partner during the AIDS crisis.

"Trauma," I repeated solemnly.

Dana gulped. "This… this is really weird."

"Black salt," I said. "How did they know it was salt? Did they taste it? Black iron. Again, how did they know? Black gravestone. The thing in common. All black. They woke up at night, in the middle of a forest. There would be no light, other than the silver moon, and that would only be if there wasn't a cloud in the sky." I pulled the notes I'd taken of the weather forecast for the days each individual had disappeared. "Daniel, 1991, clouds. Abbie Crawford, 1999, clouds. Godric McUlster, 2002, clouds. They each knew the tale of the Sluagh. It's a truth here more than where I come from, even in Glasgow. It's their truth. Their trauma."

With a look of victory, Dana stood and withdrew the recorder from her pocket. "I have proof she was real. The interview."

Dana placed the recorder on the table, turning the volume low, and pressed play. The first few audio glitches crackled before her voice made the introductions. Just as the recording returned to where Dana used the old lady's name, she paused. "Right here. She corrects me."

"Geraldine". BZZZZZT.

"Wait," said Dana, giving the recorder a tap on her palm. "Well, the next time she speaks, right after you interrupt—"

"Provided guidance," I said bitterly.

Dana returned a side-eyed glance before pressing play. *"Experienced."* BZZZZZZT.

"The fuck?"

"Do you believe me now?" I said.

Shaking her head, Dana kept playing the recording. She and I were speaking clearly through it, but any time that *Gerry* spoke, there was nothing but static.

"No, no, no, no!" said Dana so loudly that we got told off by the librarian. I wasn't overly happy with the exchange, but she had just witnessed something life changing so I hadn't the care to be an arse about it.

"Then, what now?" asked Dana, defeated.

"We go to the forest and see for ourselves."

Dana threw up her arms and snorted in derision. "Why?"

"To see if it's true."

Sunset approached as we made our way to the forest. After the library, Dana took the initiative and made her way to the shops in Glenkiln, picking up supplies; food, water, torches, and walkie talkies.

I wasn't sure what I was expecting when we got there. Most likely nothing at all – just a forest in the calm night – but that feeling of anxiety never went away, never for a second. The chance of experiencing something supernatural gave me a reason to keep going.

Passing the cottage, we took out our torches. With no streetlights to guide our way, the grey canvas of trees ahead of us was a dangerous path to tread without light. Safety was paramount when searching for ancient beings of power.

We began by following the Allt Mor stream into the hills. The tranquil melody of the twilight forest drew me in like a siren's song. Just the lapping of wind upon the pine trees and the gentle birdsong. For a moment, it makes you forget yourself – for better or worse – and lets you realise that most of humanity has forgotten what makes the world so magical.

We walked for almost an hour and still had plenty of ground to cover. Oranges and purples filled the almost full-night sky.

"We should split up," I said. "I'll head northeast, and you east. We'll try and stay within half a mile."

Dana nodded. "Urm, of course." It was the first time I heard trepidation in her voice.

Twenty minutes later, as the wind subsided and the forest went silent, a voice crackled over the walkie talkie. "Er, testing testing. One, two, three," said Dana.

"Yes," I said. "Still working. Over."

"Tell me more about yourself."

"Now is not the right time. Over."

"I know, but…" she said, sighing. "I can admit when I am a little bit scared. Alone in the woods is not a place I usually hang out."

I began to feel sympathy for her. "Fine, what do you want to—"

A figure moved between the trees. I pointed my torch through the now foggy thicket. "Who's out there?"

With the silent forest, all I could hear was my own heartbeat. Sweat dripped down my forehead.

"Matlock. Did… you see something?"

"Something?" I said, trying not to give in to a brief moment of insanity.

"Matlock… Matlock… he's after me. Help me, help!" she said, followed by crackling.

"Dana!" I yelled. "Dana, call out. Who's after you?"

"Help me, please!"

"Dana!"

The walkie talkie crackled. "God sake," I cursed. I debated throwing the walkie talkie on the ground or breaking it with my hands. I settled on biting it. Unorthodox, and a bit cliché, but I tried to deal the least amount of damage to the only device capable of reaching Dana.

Without Dana I felt isolated, and I was concerned for her safety. The woods in the dark are unsafe enough, but she'd seen *something*. It was surely all in her mind – but when you are alone and trapped, your mind can make it real.

I turned and turned, looking for a light between the branches in the distance, to seek her out. My breath quickened, my palms were clammy, and my eyes darted around manically. I was no use to her – to myself – panicked.

Taking a deep breath, I attempted to calm myself. The cold did not help; the frigid air filled my lungs and made me panic more. I wanted to run, to escape the torment, the dark sea of pines. The voices of doubt spiralled in my head, ever closer to driving me insane…

"Tay?" a voice called from the walkie talkie.

I froze, and my heart stopped.

"Tay," *she* said again. "Help me."

"I…" I babbled, barely able to speak. "Tell me where you are."

"I'm so cold."

"I know, I know, I'm coming for you."

"I'm alone," *she* said. "Save me."

The walkie talkie crackled with a bright spark. I dropped the device. Smoke billowed out from it. Had I broken it? It didn't seem possible.

In the distance, I heard a sudden cry. Navigating the twilight forest at speed was dangerous, but I threw caution to the wind, seeking out Dana in the chaos of the thicket. Pine needles whipped at my arms and legs as I batted away the branches. My hands and face felt the icy sting of the trunks as I barrelled into them, the adrenaline piloting me forward.

My mouth dried out in the cold air, cracking my lips and causing my throat to seize up. I could barely breathe. I was not a good runner, and my knees were ready to give out.

I stopped to recuperate. I had not heard a cry for a few minutes, and I looked around frantically. I tried to call out, but the lack of saliva and sheer pain in my throat meant I could barely let out a whimper.

I leant up a tree to support my exhausted limbs. My arms and legs were grazed; small tears in my clothes revealed bloody scrapes, stinging in the cold.

Another scream. Ignoring the pain once again, I took off, slower, and less confident I would make the journey. I could feel my muscles giving up, and a feeling took over me, an urge to lie down on the ground. To give in to the forest, to be a part of it.

Flickering ahead, I finally saw a light. With a deep breath, I slammed my fist into a tree and walked as fast as I could without breaking into another sprint. I was close. Whatever this was, I had to stop it.

Dana sat on the ground. Her torch sat in the dirt, its beam illuminating a tree; her walkie talkie was smoking like mine had. Her arms were wrapped around her knees.

"Dana," I said, reaching out an arm. "It's alright. I'm here."

"I thought I put it behind me. I thought I moved on. But *he* caught up. Resentment and pain."

I knelt beside her. "We'll leave. Let's get back..."

"No," she stood, wiping tears with her sleeve. "We keep going."

For the first time, I respected her.

Leaving the broken walkie talkies behind, we ventured further into the dark forest. It was bitterly cold, a stark contrast to the blazing sun during the day. It was almost a nice change. We passed through an endless sea of pine trees, the branches clawing at us from the shadows. Each movement felt like something stalking us, ready to pounce.

"I read your blog," said Dana.

"Nice to know," I said. "Always happy to meet a fan."

"Suppose it should be, considering you're not exactly the most popular folklore blogger."

"I suppose not," I said with a shrug. "Which is a shame because I have spent my life listening, researching, and experiencing other cultures—"

"And then trampling on their beliefs to earn a pretty penny."

I scoffed at that. "My mould-ridden one bedroom flat on the outskirts of Birmingham would disagree with that."

Dana squinted. "Then why do it?"

I took a moment before answering. She was a truth-seeker, like me. Both of us lived for the chance to write something provocative. But there was more to it, and after what we had both been through, I felt no need to keep it in any longer. I let out a long sigh.

"Because I need to know if there truly is something paranormal out there."

"That's admirable. Couldn't you just become a TV presenter and get a shit documentary series on Netflix?"

"It's not for the money."

"Clearly. So, what is it for?"

"My wife," I said.

I wanted to scream. To bellow out my lungs at full volume and shake the trees, causing a flock of birds to scatter from the canopy. But instead, it came out as a whimper. A true testament to what *her* memory had become.

"She died unexpectedly," I said, "Police said it was suicide, but I just knew it wasn't. I urged them to continue looking for the real cause. Murder, accident, anything. They refused."

Dana blinked, taken aback.

"I never wanted to accept that truth, so I looked for answers. The paranormal. I had it in my head that she was killed by something supernatural. A creature of the night, a ghoul, a reaver, something. But the more I dug, the further I fell into the pit. I've travelled the world looking for answers, but there are none." I swallowed hard. "There are no ghosts. No werewolves, or vampires, or chupacabras. Just broken people seeking answers. That is why I do this. Because I have to hope that one day, I will be justified in believing something else took her. Because if I stop looking, I have nothing to live for."

I breathed heavily. My legs felt like jelly as I held myself up against the tree.

Dana placed a hand on my shoulder. "I'm sorry. That must've been hard."

"It was."

We walked in silence for a while. I spent time reflecting on what I told Dana, and I assumed she was reflecting upon what she was told. I kept telling myself that there had to be something out there. That everything we'd seen had to mean something.

And there was. As if from a dream. Ahead was a mound in the centre of a clearing. Fog dared not touch its peak, instead surrounding it like a skirt. It was still dark, so the features were indistinguishable at first, but the more I stared in stunned silence, the more the picture revealed itself.

Surrounding the mound stood a fence, bent and deformed, most of its sharp spikes pointing toward the heavens. Some of the posts resembled twisted roots. Upon the incline of the mound stood many smaller stones, less than a foot tall, fashioned like a pinecone around the perimeter. At the top a tombstone stood proud, a beckoning darkness, more macabre than any creature one could imagine. It gave me a sense of dread, but also purpose.

I walked slowly toward the cemetery, my torch aimed true, in case it disappeared. Black tombstones. Black fence. I knelt and pointed the torch, revealing a line of pure black crystals surrounding the mound. I dipped my finger in it and tasted. Salt.

I made my way to the tombstones. The ghost of the old

lady had not lied. There it was. My name, written as if I had died centuries past.

But there was also *her* name. My wife's name, next to me, chiselled as an epitaph. Kindred souls. Yet somehow, I still possessed my physical form.

Footsteps walked softly behind me.

"Is this some fucking trick?" said Dana.

"I don't know."

"My name is Dana!" she yelled out in anger.

I raised a brow, confused at the non sequitur.

"My name is Dana! Can't you understand that I—" Her eyes suddenly bulged. A humanoid figure stood just outside of the cemetery. It stalked from the treeline, but did not move. It came from the fog and was in turn a part of it. No feet, but gangly arms and torso, a face stretched to its limit. I did not recognise what this thing was, but Dana stared at it with anguished familiarity.

I froze once again, but this time from confusion. "Dana, I—"

"I shouldn't have come here. I shouldn't have come here..." Dana paced back and forth, rubbing her arm until it turned red with irritation. Her anger turned to anguish that turned to pure fear. This thing was immaterial, yet she saw it for what it was, or what she perceived it to be. The forest's silence was no longer the absence of noise, but a low hum of terror stretched out across the foggy thicket.

I went to stand by her, to place an arm on her shoulder, to face this thing together. She had not experienced such a terror before and I had to be there for her, to guide her through – to remind her it was all her trauma and not real.

"Tay," *she* said from behind me.

"It's a trick," I said. "The Sluagh."

"You said it wasn't real," said Dana.

"We've made it real. *She* is here."

I turned toward *her*. Dana was fixated on her own ghostly trauma. I shook my head in disbelief. I'd seen *her* face in every reflection, but this time was different. No fog spectre like Dana's. *She* was there, in front of me, standing on solid ground, wearing *her* favourite blouse. I smelt the gooseberry perfume *she* always wore.

I let out a long breath to steady my nerves. Spittle flew out as my lips shook, betraying what I wanted to say.

"Tay, my love, come to me," *she* said.

Tears fell down my cheeks as I stood in place. "I… I can't, my love. You don't exist. It's a trick."

Her form changed after every blink. I wanted to keep my eyes open, but the tears forced me to close them.

Dana screamed behind me, tripping over the black stones. "I can't leave. I can't get out. Something is stopping me."

I knew at that moment what was to happen. The same as the victims before. Or better: a real haunting. I wanted this to be real. It meant *she* was real, that *she* didn't die in vain. That there was a truth to it. And that *she* hadn't taken *her* own life at all.

I wiped the tears away. *She* had won. A part of me would rather have been taken by the Sluagh. Then I wouldn't have to face the reality that I'd been ignorant to her suffering. I could have helped, I should have been there, not stuck in my own head, in my own fairytale. Chasing ghosts around the world allowed me to continue this lie, to never grieve what may have been the truth.

I couldn't live with the knowledge that this was all in my head.

Daring to look up, just for a second, I realised how magnificent everything was. Gaunt humanoids hung from the night sky, suspended in midair. Their bodies gangly, their fingers thin, tapering to sharp nails; their faces contorted in pain. My pain. *Our* pain.

Dana cried out behind me. "You are not my truth," she said to the masculine figure. "It took me a while to realise that. The self-hatred, the pain I brought to others. I finally came to terms with my truth. I worked hard to better myself."

I cocked my head just enough to see Dana but also keep *her* in my sight.

She stood, walking forward, toward the humanoid standing at the edge of the cemetery. Jabbing a finger toward *him*.

"You are not my truth," she said again. "You are what I left behind, what kept me prisoner in my own mind. You will not keep me prisoner anymore. I know who I am."

Dana held her position. Her conviction sent a shiver down my goosebumped body.

The humanoid dissipated into the fog, like a lost memory, drifting through the forest. Dana's legs turned to jelly as she sat down on the forest floor, wrapping herself in her arms.

She had faced her trauma. And won.

I took a deep breath. I didn't really understand what had happened at that moment. I didn't need to. Dana's trauma was hers and not mine. Whatever demons she faced, they were not new to her.

Just like mine.

Her.

The truth of *her* was as scary to me as never knowing.

I took another deep breath and turned so I could stare deeply into *her* eyes.

"It's okay if you did what they say you did," I told her "You did what was best for you. I just wish there was something I could have done to prevent it. I'm not angry about what you did. I'm just sad that I will never see your face again. And that is my burden, not yours." I let out a long exhalation.

"I love you, May," I told her. "And I need to let you go."

Her face changed. I blinked, but it stayed the same. It was her. My May. Her dirt-stained blouse, her gardening gloves she won at the county faire; her brown corduroy trousers, snagged at the hem from the overgrowth in the garden. The scent of gooseberries. That crooked smile from when she broke a tooth as a teenager. The wrinkle of her nose that I always adored. Her deep brown eyes that calmed the storm raging within me. All of it was her. The real her.

Our last day together. She'd asked me to help clear the branches and roots and weeds. Time we could have spent in the garden together on that first day of spring, when the sun finally came out and the birdsong returned. I was too busy, I told her, too busy not living in the moment, finding a way to make us money. My intentions were pure, but I would have traded it all for one more afternoon in the sun with my May.

"I love you," I said. "Be at rest."

The sun finally began to rise, bringing with it an orange and pink sky. She melted into the morning mist, carried into the air, taking the gangly figures with her.

I turned to Dana. Her smile was weak, but genuine.

We watched the sun rise over the horizon, filling light in between the pine trees and carving a path through the morning mist and mildew. Where we stood was no longer a black cemetery, but a mound of moss and mushrooms formed into a circle at the top. It felt ancient and powerful. Butterflies fluttered over the mound, filling the sky with colour and life, like a fluttering rainbow, and at the end, the prize. Not of gold, but forgiveness.

I closed my eyes, and a weight lifted. The soft wind rustled the trees, and the morning birdsong felt like a symphony. The cold air lapped upon my cheeks, and for a second I swore it felt like a hand, cupping my face. Soft fingers, but a calloused palm.

There is magic in the world. We are all just too traumatised to see it.

Something Peculiar

from

Under the Similitude
of a Dream

"…doodles of monkeys playing fiddles and tambours…"

IN THE week, the Narrator tramps from farmstead to hamlet to manor to town, bowed beneath his heavy pack, plying his trade, mending the pans and pots and ladles brought out to him. Sometimes he'll stop at some olden place, an ancient crossing of the ways or a humped barrow, set down his gear and watch the wights flit about for a time. On Sundays, he preaches – in barns, in taverns, in blacksmiths' forges, from the black and hollow stump of a blasted oak. The throngs that gather hang on his every word. He tells them of the Celestial City, of the way there, of the relief from strife and want awaiting those ready to tread that hard path. All who hear him renounce the worldly, the carnal – dream evermore of those gleaming walls, those gold-paved streets.

At night, he becomes a small red devil, with leathery wings, a slug's horns, the eyes of a squid, and the proboscis of a blowfly, and flaps from grand house to hovel and flits in through open casements or seeps through panes of glass or hung animal skins, and sits astride sleepers' chests, slopping his mouthparts down over their faces to suck up their dreams.

Bethany lay awake, unable to sleep, partly because it was so close and clammy, unseasonable weather for October

– it had been so hot that week that small birds, sparrows, starlings, and blackbirds, had been falling out of the air, hearts burst – and partly because she kept turning over and over in her head how she'd died, killed by brigands after her tinker's wares, who'd come yowling out of the deep gloom of Harrow Woods, on a moonless night, as she'd trudged an ancient trackway, making for home, and set upon her with their cudgels and darkly glinting knives. The poor choices that had led to this brutal end weighed on her – if only she'd spent the night at the inn she'd passed as dusk was drawing in, had not begrudged the small handful of coin; if only she'd traded her good copper kettle for the Chinese rocket the old woman who lived in a hovel in the Mare Marsh had offered her, perhaps she might have been able to put the thieves to flight. But what really irked is that she'd neglected to save, lost an evening's play. She could feel the tension in her neck and shoulders, and her hands prickled.

The following day at work she was tired and sullen. She taught Literature at the local higher education institution, a place that had gained university status full of promise and good intentions in the early '90s, but which by then was moribund, mired in scandal and with falling standards and recruitment. She'd entered her post fresh from completing a PhD and filled with enthusiasm, at a time when student numbers were still healthy, only for a crisis to hit higher education a few years into her career. Still, she generally liked her students, small though the classes were, and she enjoyed teaching the idiosyncratic selection of texts she'd chosen for her modules. She thought she'd not much longer be able to dodge redundancy, so generally threw herself into sessions, determined to enjoy the time she had left; she didn't know what she'd do when she lost her job, but doubted, pressures on the sector being what they were, she'd find a position at another university. But that day she couldn't be bothered, though the session was one of her favourites – discussing poems and novels inspired by dreams. So she was short with the class, responded to one student's perfectly sensible question with only a withering look, which made the girl cry. She rushed through her presentation and sent the group off early, then sat slumped at the desk at the front of the room, her head in her hands. The Education lecturer teaching the next session in the space found her there, asked if anything was wrong. She shook her head, shrugged. 'Been a long day, that's all.' It was not yet lunchtime.

He hangs, the Narrator, high up in the belfry of a ruined church, amid the rustling of pigeons in their untidy nests, the stink of their shit, looking down on the roofs of the town through the slats of the luffers. Hangs upside down from a noose tied round one ankle, jerking and swinging like a pendulum at the end of his rope, and sets the town dreaming. But he also feeds on their dreams, battening on their fear and yearning, lust and misery, the charged scenes their hippocampi shit into their brainpans. The young girl who sees herself lapping a sweet nectar from the tear ducts of her preacher. The boy who is paraded through the streets, dressed only in a praying mantis mask, a stinking thing made of real chitin, while the women of the town smear honey on his limbs. The seamstress who unstitches her own hide and slips from it supple and slick like a thing newborn. The troubadour who plays on his lute a tune so bewitching that all who hear it are compelled to dance till they drop. The grey mare who slowly sinks into a mire, every shudder of her limbs dragging her down.

'Can I get a sausage roll and a jam doughnut, sweetmouth?' The man was old enough to be Jessamine's father or even grandfather, and was ugly and running to fat besides, with horribly soft hands, lank hair and a wispy moustache, but seemed to have no shame leering openly at them. They didn't mind when people called them 'sweetheart' or 'darling', but 'beautiful' and 'gorgeous' turned their stomach. And 'sweetmouth' had actually made them retch. But they choked down their disgust and taking up a pair of tongs put the man's order into two small paper bags, handed them over, took his payment. They let out a pent-up breath when he left the shop, though.

Jess didn't really mind working in the chain bakers on the High Street. The heat and the fug of grease in the air never seemed to give them spots – this was a nightmare for some of the girls they worked with who had to wear thicker and thicker layers of foundation as their skin erupted. And they liked that their dark ringlets always smelled cloying, of frying doughnuts and baking sausage rolls, no matter how often they washed their hair, liked that it put off boys in clubs, though hopefully after they'd already bought them a shot of something, generally sambuca – sambuca was their favourite. It wasn't necessarily a job they'd have chosen, but it was money for rent, on the room in the place they shared with a couple of other young people. Besides, they were still in their teens, even if twenty was looming, and there was plenty of time. Perhaps they'd go back to college. Or study literature at university – that was their dream. They loved to read. Especially Victorian novels. They imagined themselves as Jane Eyre, with a dark, plain, and pinched, if elfish countenance, though in truth they had a winning open face. They shared short clips of them talking about their favourites on social media, but got more snide comments than likes or followers. They'd no illusions about that era, knew that for someone of their class, life would have been cheap and likely short, but they dreamed of themself as a Pre-Raphaelite model, androgynous features, if long flowing hair, catching a chill in an old tin bath or coughing up blood, dying of consumption.

Victorian novels were Jess's favourite. But they loved Jane Austen too and the Gothic novels of Ann Radcliffe. And it was an even earlier book that had first got them into reading – an illustrated children's edition of *The Dream Vision of the Pious Tinker* their mum had found in a second-hand bookshop and given to them when they were a child. They'd treasured it, would lose themself in the pictures, foundered with the wayfarer in the marsh, cowered from the lions chained outside the opulent house, battled with the dragon demon, sank into despair in the dungeons of the giant's castle, and rejoiced to finally sight, on the summit of a steep mountain, the walls and battlements, the spires, turrets, and gilded cupolas of the heavenly city. The artist had worked with woodcut prints, had chosen to depict these scenes in blocks of black, red, and gold, and Jess saw them still – vivid, stark, cycling like a slide show – when they closed their eyes, though they'd not seen the book in years. They guessed their grandparents had donated it when they'd cleared out the house after their mum had died, but since their grandparents wouldn't speak to them anymore, they supposed they'd never find out. They'd looked for it in all the charity shops and second-hand bookshops in town, with no luck, and internet searches only turned up more famous illustrated editions.

But it was this that had drawn Jess into the game after they'd read a review of it online. It had appealed to their memory of the book and to their sense of the strange. So they'd saved up a bit and bought it.

They were quickly hooked, soon spent most of their free time playing. Stopped going out save to work and to the town library for books, though even that was less often than before – they spent time in the game when they'd usually have been reading. At first their flatmates were concerned, tried to drag them away from their PC, get them to socialise, but after a while they gave up, and Jess spent more and more time in their room, glued to their monitor. The game's weird procedural sprawl entranced them. You began always in the City of Destruction and had to find your way out of that place – a sprawl of half-timbered buildings, lurching to butt heads, a stench of rotting vegetable peelings, horseflesh, and cinnamon. One run you might be a novitiate, in a sackcloth cowl, hiding in a barrel on the cart of a maker of mead who was hauling his wares to a tavern somewhere outside the walls. On another, you were a minstrel lulling the guards at one of the city gates with the buzzing drones of your peasant's lyre. On yet another, a pilgrim, bent double beneath your bulky pack, cupping your hands to beg for alms. Then, once you'd got out of the city, not an easy thing at first, but simple enough once you were used to it, the game opened up, and Jess found that things were never the same twice. One evening they were a knight doing battle with the demons who'd possessed the monks of a Gothic abbey and were harrowing the folk of the land about. They'd put nearly all the fiends to the sword when they were attacked and torn limb from limb by the creature the abbot had become, a writhing mass of vegetable tubers clad in a brown habit. The next night they were a tavern wench, forced to dance on tables for jeering men, who ended up putting hemlock in the mead and swinging from the gallows for it.

Then Jess was a bibliomancer who lived in a hovel in the middle of dark woods. They just had the one book they worked with, an illuminated manuscript of Geoffrey of Monmouth's *De gestis Britonum*, bound in calf-leather the colour of catshit. How they'd come by such a rare and valuable volume, and how they'd held on to it, no one knew. The pages were translucent in places from their greases, from their obsessive handling of it. They couldn't read Latin, but loved the drolleries in the margins: doodles of monkeys playing fiddles and tambours; a hare beheading a hunting dog with an executioner's axe; frogs jousting, riding atop snails; maidens looking lasciviously up at a tree fruited with drooping cocks; a naked monk with a bellows up his arse. They couldn't read, but performed their divinations by interpreting the shape of the cursive on the page on which the book fell open, and those who visited them seeking their fortunes couldn't read either, so this worked. They had long blue-grey hair, though they were still young, with a small mouth.

One day a nobleman came to Jess seeking knowledge of his fate – he wished to know if he was destined one day to be king. They read the book, told his future as given to them by their mantic art, but he didn't like what he heard, so hung them by their blue hair from a tree branch and flayed them alive. From their tanned hide he had a jerkin sewed, which he wore, thinking it would bring him luck, but it just itched and nipped at him, so in the end he threw it out on his manor's midden. The manuscript he kept, because he like one of the pictures, of a maid lifting her skirts to frighten a demon with her nethermouth.

Out on the midden, their skin put down roots into the dung and slop, drawing strength from it, then budded forth a babe, the dark green of a yew's needles with eyes the red of its berries. This babe grew swift into a beautiful young thing with prehensile fingers and toes, who one warm summer's night climbed the ivy clinging to the walls of the noble's manor, in through the open casement of his bedroom window, and finding him touching himself while looking at that picture of the maid, throttled him with their pine-blue hair. Then slowly ate the pages of the book, one after another, and nourished by the words, grew till they blotted out the sun, and the age of giants began anew. This was an ending, though whether a good or a bad one Jess found it hard to say. Of course, it wasn't the true ending.

That any game could just appear on the various PC and console storefronts one day, without anyone in the industry knowing anything about the studio or developers that made it, was strange enough. That it was so immersive, so compelling, it had, with only word of mouth, no marketing, become an overnight cult, was truly bizarre. But its oneiric visuals were so vivid and its writing so frenetic yet subtle, the first few players who'd picked it up on a whim, perhaps hooked by the title or cover art, which appeared to be an original oil painting, in the Dutch Renaissance style, of demons and folk in cowled robes dancing through a blasted landscape, had felt driven to tell others about it, write fervent reviews online. How could what was presumably a small team have pulled off something so gripping and fully realised? True, the UI was clunky and laborious (but that really just enhanced the feel of a brutal, unforgiving world), the graphical fidelity poor (though the hallucinatory art direction more than made up for that), but still, the thing was unfeasible.

Burgholt had been commissioned by a well-known online gaming mag to review it soon after release. Initially he'd found it tortuous and dull, had considered turning down the assignment, but then, after a good run, was sucked in. He'd kept on playing and discovered the other bizarre thing about the game, which others online were beginning to comment on – that every player's experience was radically different, that it apparently had no end. It seemed to be an emergent narrative rewriting itself as people engaged with it, pulling from some dark algorithmic illogic, but how that was possible, how it could have programmed, no one could guess. Online play enabled another layer of chaos and cruelty – clips of streamers sabotaging other gamers' playthroughs went viral. The game was a roguelite: deaths were permanent and meant restarting, but some elements of progression carried through to subsequent runs. It was really less about winning, though, than simply enduring – a fever dream from which you couldn't wake. But rumours began to circulate on internet forums of a Celestial City, a place of eternal joy and rest, whose glittering walls, atop a steep mountain, players had glimpsed far off in the distance.

Burgholt had slowly grown obsessed with the game. He realised just how much he was in thrall one night when he emerged blinking from a long session having died in some way that was obscure to him. It was the witching hour, but his girlfriend, Mary, was awake in the living room, cradling their infant daughter, Nancy.

'Burg,' she said. 'What are you thinking?'

He sat down next to her on the sofa. 'I know. Sorry!'

'Maybe it was fine when it was just the two of us, but… You've got to take a bit of responsibility.'

'I will, I swear. It's this review, well…'

'Just file and move on. You're not getting paid to spend this long on it.'

Burgholt nodded. 'Sure. It's only that it's a work of art, you know? Just now I was in this place that flickered between an opulent seventeenth-century mansion and its ruins. The house was thronged with folk dressed in shimmering satin gowns and rich doublets and breeches, and wearing elaborate, monstrous masks. The shell was empty save for two teenagers, in modern clothes, jeans and hoodies, who were huffing nitrous oxide from lurid balloons, sitting in a circle of salt—'

Just then Nancy woke and began to keen, going red in the face and clenching her little fists.

'Now look what you've done! You've set her off. And I'd just managed to get her back to sleep.'

'Sorry! Didn't mean to.'

'Okay. Well, I'll take her into bed, try to calm her down. But you'll have to sleep out here on the sofa.'

Burgholt nodded, watched as they went into the bedroom, Mary dandling and hushing the baby.

But he didn't sleep, instead started a new run, tried to find that house again. But this time, when he got to where he thought it had been, he found instead a shrine built from massy bones, yellowing ribs curving overhead, the lintel a huge jawbone. Inside, on a lump of green sandstone, was a black and shrivelled thing like a slug, but calcified brittle. The Narrator's tongue, an object worthy of veneration.

The following afternoon, Burgholt was walking down the high street in town, the smell of doughnuts frying in his nostrils, the music of a barrel organ in his ears, when he became aware that a boy, no more than eleven or twelve, had come up alongside him. He glanced down and saw the child staring back. Burgholt frowned, but walked on, now a little faster. Grinning, the boy continued to keep pace. Then said, low but distinct, with both a sneer and threat, 'Thy saints take pleasure in her stones and favour the dust thereof.'

Burgholt now peered at the boy. He was wearing archaic garb – a smock and leather breeches – and covered in dirt from head to toe.

'What?' Burgholt said, more to himself than to the boy.

Who then began shouting to passers by. 'Urgh, what are you doing? Don't touch me!'

People were starting to look. Burgholt, shaken, backed off, walked away, but the boy kept shouting after him. 'Filthy pervert! I'm just a child.'

He didn't mention it to Mary, but the encounter unsettled him for days.

Jess had taken on extra work – a nighttime shift at a warehouse – in order to buy parts to upgrade their rig – the game had fairly hefty system requirements for an indie title, and they wanted to be able to run it at full specs. They had started streaming, something they'd never had any interest in before, and straight away found an obsessive community and fans who hung on their runs – somehow they were consistently able to get further in than most others, whether due to RNG good fortune or some element of skill they weren't aware of, they weren't sure. But one afternoon they were streaming, playing through an area they'd encountered a few times before, a forest of living trees that snatched at the player with writhen branches, when they burst into a glade full of moonlight where stood a living statue, a stern-faced woman in porphyry, garbed in a cloak of green jasmine. It was a boss fight, but one with a gimmick: the jasmine bloomed when the player's shadow fell on it, and the statue could only be damaged where the flowers were open. Which meant trying always to stay between the statue and the moon, which was not easy, as it whirled around the arena. But Jess still had half an eye on the chat and saw, among the flurry running down the right side of their monitor – encouragement, critiques of their gameplay, and sexist and transphobic jibes – messages posted by someone with the user name 'the_narrat0r'. There was nothing overtly threatening in them, but they were strange, and somehow pointed:

when st0r1es begin to leak
u will c in ur smol town in the centaur of the countree
in the centaur hahaha ;)
in a festooned cat's skull, holding a lyre
u'll c the leeeking st0r1es

Distracted, Jess dropped their guard, and the statue managed to get them by the throat and swing them round the clearing, before opening a gaping maw, and taking off the top of their head with marble incisors.

When Bethany's university announced the inevitable redundancies, she fully expected and even hoped hers would be one of the jobs affected. When it wasn't, she applied for the voluntary severance scheme, planning to use the payout to retrain. But when she was knocked back, lacking savings, she'd no choice but to stay on, though her heart was no longer in it. Her lectures, now more and more on texts from the canon and outside her specialisms, as she took over modules from staff members who'd been let go and the course was rationalised, were increasingly lacklustre and ill prepared, and she took lazy shortcuts with her marking and administration.

But she did throw herself into the game, determined to find Mount Zion and climb to the Celestial City. As she'd moved for the job, she was far from her close friends, who were anyway a bit scattered now, and beginning to settle down, start families. She enjoyed socialising with her colleagues, but that was rare – they were mostly a bit older and busy with their lives. So she didn't have much else to do. And she found more and more people were playing, despite the game's obscurity and brutal systems. Online interactions became quite hectic, and it came up in conversation on a surprising number of the desultory dates she went on with men she'd met on apps. It was from one of these she heard tell of the mysterious Narrator.

The date was at a wine bar in town. The man, whose name was Peter, had seemed nice enough when they were messaging each other, but still Beth didn't have high hopes for the evening; she'd basically written off all single men in the age bracket she connected with, which was about ten years older – men her own age tended to be looking for women quite a bit younger. But actually Peter was nice – thoughtful and genuinely interested in finding out more about her. He told her he was a solicitor, though he wouldn't say much more about it: 'Far too dull.' But he wanted to hear all about her work and the novels she was teaching – he was a reader, which was rare. He even commiserated when Beth moaned about the terrible conditions in Higher Education, seemed to share a fair amount of her politics. And he was good looking, she thought, with kind eyes.

They'd drunk cocktails and most of a bottle of wine, so Beth couldn't recall who brought up it up first, but then they were talking about the game, exchanging tips and discussing secrets.

'Have you come across the Interpreter?' Peter asked.

Beth was munching on an olive, fished out the stone, set it down on a napkin. 'No, I don't think so.'

'It's a man dressed in a tweed three-piece suit and sitting in a wing chair. I found him in a dusty parlour lit only by the guttering candle he held in his hand. He seemed to be peering at me intently, though couldn't see his eyes – the flickering flame danced on the round lenses of the spectacles he wore. On the walls of the room was hung a series of allegorical woodcuts which he told me to look at. In one a man sat in a cage, looking downcast, fettered by irons. In another a stately palace blazed. I can't now recall the rest.' Peter paused, took a sip of his wine.

'Where did you find him?'

'Not far out from the City of Destruction. There was a marsh, then a sandstone scarp. If you've not encountered the Interpreter yet, are you still carrying around your burden?'

Beth took a sip of her wine. 'No. I was relieved of it by a porter I met on the road, called Watchful, who had impossible strength, and carried many packs on his back.'

'The Interpreter showed me one other picture, a little engraving he had in a locket on a chain, which he kept in his fob. It was of a stout jowly man with long curly hair, sparse whiskers, and a little goatee, who was wearing coat and breeches and walked a path, weighed down by a tinker's pack. Floating above his head was a crown of gold, from which rays darted. This, the Interpreter said, was the Narrator, though he wouldn't be drawn into telling me more.'

At the end of the evening, Beth went back with Peter to his flat in town. It was a cold night, so she snuggled against him as they walked. When they got into his sparely but expensively furnished flat, she thought they'd go straight through to his bedroom, but instead he took her into his study, switched on his PC.

'I wanted to show you something. I've got a really good run going.'

The computer booted up, then Peter ran the game, loaded his save. He pointed at his avatar who was clad in shining robes and had an angelic countenance.

'I was given a clothing set called the Celestial Garment by an NPC named Turn-away I found in a cave I passed by. It causes people to trust me, so I've been leading players, telling them I know the road to Mount Zion, into a trap. I've ensnared so many this way. Look, I'll show you.'

Beth, who'd been perched on his office chair with him, stood up, backed away, peered at him. 'Why?'

'Well, it's fun you know. And prevents people from making it to the Celestial City before me.'

Beth smiled. Then, before Peter could stop her, stabbed out with her finger and switched off his PC.

'What are you doing?'

'I hope your save gets corrupted, you prick.'

Then she turned, grabbed her things, and left, leaving Peter fuming. On the walk home she shuddered, hunched herself into her coat, and vowed not to go on any more dates through apps.

But she couldn't get Peter's words about the Narrator out of her head. So took to posting on internet forums where players of the game shared tips and theories about its lore. And there read more and more cryptic references to the character and his significance.

By the time Mary, who was really very patient, had had enough and left to go and stay with her parents, taking Nancy with her, Burgholt had lost weeks, months to the game, hardly even pausing to eat, drink, or sleep, sitting in his gaming chair at his computer, his office a stale fug of sweat, ignoring freelance work coming in, irking good, reliable employers. He didn't hear the sound of the door slamming over the squealing of swine in his headphones, so it was only when his run later ended, broken on a wheel in the dungeons of Doubting Castle, and he went to take a piss, that he noticed there was no sound of crying, and that Mary's things were gone. There was a note on the kitchen counter – he crumpled it up and threw it in the bin without reading it. Then he shrugged, opened a bottle of wine, swigged from it, and took it back with him into his office, where he started another run. It wasn't till hours later, when he died again, clubbed to death by homunculi amid the heaped middens which were revealed when you looked at Vanity Fair through the Lens of Verity, that he sank his head in his hands and wept and shuddered. When his crying jag waned though, he felt as numb and hollow as before, if hungry. So he got up to go and make some toast. Switching on the light in his office, he saw that a ram's skull, with involute horns, swagged with fruit and vegetable peelings, and looking like some fetish, sat in the centre of the room on the carpet.

The narrator has become a giant, fed by dreams, and has built a fortress on a hill, with walls of fear, lust, joy, grief, shame, anxiety, and rage, all leeched from the amygdalae of his many congregations. He broods within it, stories leaking from his every orifice, his every pore, a spate of stories flowing down the slopes to flood the land about.

One night, a couple of weeks after the weird messages had popped up on their stream, Jess was walking home late, the witching hour, after a night out clubbing, having finally given in to the urgings of some old friends. They'd surprised themselves by getting drunk and taking a pill, and actually having a good time. They were grinning ear to ear as they walked, and there were flary coronas haloing the streetlights. Then they happened to glance into an alley between two houses and saw, in the gloom, a young man, topless in spite of the chill, ghastly pale and starveling, who wore as a mask the skull of a cat, from which colourful ribbons streamed. In his hands, he clutched a toy harp on which he plucked a plangent air that cut through the nighttime sounds of drunken yelling, traffic, and the wails of sirens. Jess was mesmerised, but then heard a skittish pawing of hooves, saw dappled flanks, a powerful croup, and turned and ran on, heart pounding, not stopping till they reached the front door of their house and let themselves in.

In late winter, the university finally found a way to get rid of Beth. So she told her family and few remaining friends she would hole up, speak to a career consultant, work on her CV. But instead she played the game, and went further and further down the rabbit holes of theory and lore. And it wasn't just her. The game had by now become a genuine craze in spite of everything, its difficulty, its obscurity, its weirdness. The tabloids even began to print sensational headlines talking about adults playing in nappies, broken families, shut-ins, even gamers dying of thirst because they couldn't tear themselves away. Beth wasn't at that stage, but she couldn't deny she was obsessed. It seemed so crucial, though – to play the game, eventually to find her way to the foot of Mount Zion, begin her ascent.

Then one night she was playing late, immersed in a run. She'd found a couple of potent artefacts early, a wooden begging bowl and a broom, and they had carried her through some difficult encounters. Then in a stroke of luck, she was able to buy, from a tinker, the Shield of Faith, and with that, some well-timed dodges, and a magical arbalest, she was able to defeat the demonic dragon, Apollyon, for the first time. Then, as her character needed to recover her strength, she rested in a hayloft an NPC had assured her was safe. But she had her throat cut by a thief as she slept, which made her nearly smash her controller in frustration. Then she went to sleep herself, and lay in till mid-morning the next day. When she was finally woken, by the sound of some junk mail coming through her letter box, her scalp itched, and when she put her hand to her head, she found there was straw in her hair.

That drove her onto the forums, where she asked a question – though keeping things vague lest anyone thought her mad. Checking back half an hour later, she found she'd had lots of responses, many of them unhinged or sneering. But one, from u/lizzzie_s1Doll, said simply, 'I think I know what you're talking about. DM me.' And another, from u/Burgholt1978, read, 'It's been happening to me too. I don't know what to make of it.'

Grown fat on the spoils, the Narrator sleeps beneath the stagnant waters of a marl pit, a gross lump of corpse wax in which lurid viscera can faintly be seen.

Beth, Jess, and Burgholt arranged a co-op session for the next day. They were determined to reach Mount Zion, thought that might be the way to release the game's hold over them. With their combined experience and permanent upgrades, they felt they might have a chance.

During the easier early stages, they chatted on their headsets. They were at first staggered to discover they were all from the small town in the middle of the country where the pious tinker had written his dream narrative in prison. But then realised it made sense.

'What do you think's happening?' Beth asked as the three of them worked together to trip Giant Despair with a rope stretched across his path, then roll his insensible bulk into a chasm. 'Where do you think this came from?'

Burgholt sniffed, said, 'I don't know. But I think it has to do with the Narrator.'

'I do too,' Jess said. 'I don't know what he is and can't guess at his motives, but he's responsible somehow, I'm sure.'

'So what should we do?'

'Reach the Celestial City. The answers will be there.'

On that run things ended in a fly-tipping spot on the edge of a bluebell woods, among the carcasses of old TVs, fridges, and two rusting campervans, when savage imps fell on them from out of the branches. But with a lot of skill and a bit of luck, on the next attempt the three of them made it further than any of them had before. It took hours, but most of their talk was about what they were doing, enemies they were fighting, puzzles they were solving. But in a few more tranquil moments – making their way across a meadow where sheep and goats grazed, rowing across a reservoir – they chatted about some of the stranger things that could be found in the game. One of these was something Burgholt had seen when he'd ventured far off the road to Mount Zion, all the way to the distant coast.

'A peasant there told me it was a goose-tree, a strange thing with a thick black fleshy trunk off which small growths sprouted, all tipped with a flower a bit like a mussel shell. I watched it for a good while, and a couple of times one of these flowers opened up, and a goose flew out and whooped up into the sky.'

Jess took her hands from mouse and keyboard to clap. 'I've not seen that, but I know what it's based on! There was an old legend that goose barnacles were the larval stage of the barnacle goose.'

'Weird.'

'But it was probably only something thought up so goose could be served during periods of fasting.'

'Once,' said Beth, 'I was killed by another player who dropped a rock on me. He could fly because he had a goose attached, by a stalk, to the top of his head.'

'Damn,' said Burgholt. 'To think I might have just missed out on flying. Perhaps that would have been the run when I made it to the Celestial City.'

'It doesn't matter,' said Jess, 'because we're going to make it this time.'

And they almost did. After many arduous struggles, they gained a hill called Mount Clear where some shepherds minded their flock. One of them offered Jess a look through his 'Perspective Glass', a kind of telescope, and from there they could see all the way to Mount Zion and the Celestial City, could see its cupolas, minarets, and gilded onion domes fretted from the rose of dusk, could see its walls studded with pearls and gemstones, its streets paved with gold. It didn't seem far off. They all thought they'd made it, but as they walked in that direction, Mount Zion seemed to recede always into the distance. Eventually they came to a wide river. It seemed sluggish, so they decided to swim across, but that was deceptive, there were strong and fast undercurrents, and all three of them were pulled downstream to a waterfall, where they were thrown over and dashed to pieces on the rocks below.

The next day, Beth went out to the local supermarket to pick herself up some food. The streets were eerily quiet. On the way back, weighed down by carrier bags filled with microwaveable meals and cans of premixed gin and tonic, not looking where she was going, she almost walked into someone. Seeing his feet before her, she looked up. He ran to fat, wore old-fashioned clothing, filthy breeches and a coat, and had long, unkempt hair, a thin moustache, and a little beard. On his back was a huge pack, from which hung tools, and kettles, pots, and pans, which set up a shivaree when he moved.

He smiled benignly. 'You must be Beth.'

Beth, terrified, just nodded.

'I hope you're keeping to the strait and narrow path, Beth? You can probably guess what happens to those who stray.'

And with that he trudged off, clattering. Beth jogged as fast as she could, laden down as she was, to get back to her flat.

When she got in, she straight away messaged Jess and Burgholt.

It was well known you couldn't mod the game. Decompile the code and there was no logic to it – it was just a series of cryptic phrases that read more like formulas in some arcane rite than any recognisable programming language – Jess, who was an experienced modder, had tried. But when they'd looked through the 'Perspective Glass', they'd realised it might be a key. After that last unsuccessful run, they spent hours poring over code, trying to locate the asset for the item. Once they'd found it, they realised it suggested a particular operation that could be applied to other game assets, so they scoured through till they found what they presumed to be the code for the Celestial City. It read:

```
$greatwen, recede, recede, recede! z10n() {
    for my part, ive never been moved by the stories, the
    cold sweat on my brow, nor the bitter smell of the city,
    nor the glister of 10nd0n in my nostrils, and i imagined
    he was through;
        there are a number of sites open in this world that
        are either completely different from what we know,
        or are completely collapsed by our species, stretching
        back over a billion years
        they have been warped so much that they resemble
        slabs of wood cut from twisted plastic, much as we
        have had to do with burns on a carowering horse or
        in the case of the shrike, in the presence of all but
        the most devoted following;
        }
```

Transformed by the operation, this weird code yielded something much more straightforward, two numbers, one negative, with multiple decimal places. It took Jess a moment to work out what she was looking at, but then she realised: coordinates, latitude and longitude. And only a few moments longer to pinpoint the location – somewhere in the countryside a bit of a walk from any road, a few miles south of the town in the middle of the country where she lived – the town where it had all started. She messaged Beth and Burgholt.

They met at a carpark in the centre of town – Burgholt had offered to drive them out to the site. It was an awkward first meeting – three loners by habit driven to further isolation by the yoke of the game. There was no sign of anyone on the streets, though the windows of some of the flats in the block that overlooked the carpark flickered with a grainy light.

They drove out and parked in a lay-by as close as they could to the coordinates, then climbed a fence and set off across a field. Overhead kites circled, piping shrill, and grey clouds scudded away to the west. They walked a dirt track running beside a sluggish brook. Stunted alder, willow, and hawthorn were strung out along the course of the stream, roots and low branches like snares across the path. On either side were swathes of coarse, waist-high grasses; ahead, a boggy stretch, then a gentle rise to the ancient village of Elstow, the squat tower of the abbey there jutting up like a rotten tooth; and behind, a sprawling complex of warehouses all painted light blue fading to white, so they blended into the sky. The way was flat, but the ground underfoot claggy, making the going hard, and though it was April, it was muggy, and they soon had to take off their jackets and carry them slung over their arms.

Nearing the coordinates, they came out of a copse of beech and elm into a meadow of long grass and cow parsley. A throng processed across this field, pilgrims in drab robes of sackcloth, but with flowers in their hair, the trumpet blooms of bindweed and mallow. Each had the brittle skull of a different small bird stuck to the middle of their forehead with a dollop of yellow fat – Beth, Jess, and Burgholt saw the skulls of a robin, a parakeet, a jackdaw, a hoopoe, and many others for which they had no name. The pilgrims sang and danced ungainly as they went – one churned a hurdy gurdy, another sawed at a fiddle. Beth, Jess, and Burgholt fell in with them.

Before long the parade came to a barn, a modern building of breeze block and corrugated iron, and gathered round the open doorway. Neither Beth, Jess, nor Burgholt could make anything out in the gloom within, but they heard, loud and carrying, the sound of preaching.

Then a brindled cow wandered out, full udder swaying. She lifted her massy skull to low, then stood with it hanging down, jaw open. On her lolling tongue was a city – spires and minarets, cupolas and gilded onion domes, gemstone-studded walls, and streets, paved with gold and thronged with folk who wanted for nothing.

Something Peculiar

from

Tim Major

Urchin Barren

"…as if she were looking inside a cracked skull…"

EVEN THE car park was on a slope. Billie checked the handbrake twice before exiting the Toyota, then briefly considered searching for small stones to act as chocks behind the rear wheels. She shook her head and opened the boot. Pressburger leapt out, yapping, chasing his tail in celebration of being freed.

She took from the boot of the car a slim rucksack. Her assistant, Antony, was always reliable, so she didn't need to check the contents.

"Come on, Press," she said. Pressburger snapped to her heels obediently.

The parked cars looked as though they'd been there for a while. One had a wheel clamped, another a side window missing, and the bin bag that had been used to replace it was ripped and now sputtered in the wind like a frayed flag. The cars were green with algae. It must be the sea air.

A narrow cobbled lane descended sharply from the hilltop car park. Beside it were sporadic steps for pedestrians, but Billie walked in the centre of the lane. She hadn't seen a car in motion since she'd left the dual carriageway.

The sky was grey and heavy. The thick clouds were like fat waves about to break.

Billie studied the buildings. The weathering of the large, soil-coloured stones had eroded all sharp edges.

Some walls had been whitewashed to protect them against the elements, but in many places the paint itself had succumbed.

It wouldn't do. The place wouldn't have looked anything like this in 1905.

For once, Antony had made an error. Given her own workload, she had to trust the shortlists he drew up. She couldn't afford to spend time visiting locations that were of no use to her.

Still, the cramp hadn't yet left her thighs, and Pressburger needed a long walk before he'd agree to hunker down in the back of the car again. Besides, in the past there had been instances when ignoring her initial impressions had reaped rewards. Fountains Abbey had been singularly unsuited to filming the castle scenes for *Knight Errant*, but the folly she'd discovered within its grounds had stuck in her mind, and years later she'd deployed it for a pivotal scene in a period drama that had come away with a couple of Baftas.

Anyway, she wasn't here only to see the buildings. The script of *The Mariner* specified dozens of beach scenes. The trouble with beaches was that it was impossible to get the feel of them by browsing images online. In the coming months, she ought to visit as many as possible in order to build a mental Rolodex of north-eastern coastal areas. At least it would keep Pressburger happy.

The buildings became even more dilapidated towards the foot of the slope. The whitewash was discoloured and had crumbled so much that the walls appeared like sheer cliffs strewn with bird shit. Billie stopped to look through a hole where a stone had fallen out, and to her surprise she saw through the gap the curved work surface of a modern kitchen, a wide Aga with a fashionable red kettle on its hob.

It occurred to her that she hadn't yet seen a soul.

The road opened to a wide area. There was the sea, denser grey than the clouds. To one side were heaped dozens of crab and lobster pots in disrepair, their nets snapped, their doors yawning open. Pressburger made exploratory sniffs, then abandoned them. Opposite the pile was a wooden fishing boat in no better condition. Two of its slats lay on the cobbles, their ends rotted.

Yes, the beach remained Billie's only hope. She descended a stone ramp that led downwards. Pressburger yelped, chased after nothing. Billie slung her rucksack off her shoulders and fished for the ball Antony had put there. She tossed it and Pressburger lost his mind.

The beach was visible for a mile or so, and appeared to continue around an outcrop which was shaped like a Roman nose. The sand was peppered with pebbles, and the outgoing tide had left streaks of different shades, like sedimentary layers of rock, interrupted only by a curved line of bright green seaweed.

It was ugly. Had she any use for ugliness at this time? No.

Her walking boots sank with each step. She frowned and bent to touch the ground. It was stony and hard. Why would it yield under her weight? She made a mental note to instruct Antony to allocate more time to the gym, despite his insistence that she had no need of it. She had noticed how he looked at her.

She watched Pressburger dart around this most unsuitable location. The low clouds were impressive, but even if she were scouting for a horror film this area lacked something – and she had no horrors on the slate anyway. *The Mariner* required beauty, and the fantasy TV shows for which she scouted required majesty, and this beach had neither of those qualities.

Something lying upon the sand caught her eye. At first she took it to be a smooth, brilliantly white stone, but when she examined it she saw curved lines and indentations that reminded her of the stitching of a baseball. Spilling from a central cleft was a mass of hairlike spines. It must be some sort of marine life.

Tentatively, she picked it up. It was hard and nestled neatly between the knuckles of her hand.

Far away, Pressburger barked. Billie looked up, shielding her eyes. The dog was watching her.

She gasped as the thing in her hand pulsed, making her fingers flex.

She stared at it. Was it still alive? She saw no suggestion of movement.

Her fingers flexed again. The smooth shell didn't betray any sign of motion.

An image came to mind of something trapped in there. Something creeping out of that cleft.

It pulsed again – or at least her hand did. Its rhythm became regular. Spasms travelled down Billie's arm.

She dropped the creature. It hit a stone. Its shell cracked. Bile filled Billie's mouth.

It was like a skull. As if she were looking inside a cracked skull. Within the dark interior Billie caught a glimpse of a tongue-like frond the sickly colour of polenta. Around it was a mass of gleaming dark orbs.

She couldn't stop staring. And she couldn't stand up, for fear of passing out.

"Roe," a rasping voice said.

Billie turned her head to see a large woman, perhaps in her late seventies, who wore a dust-coloured hessian poncho that hung all the way to her knees. Below it her legs were bare and speckled with coarse, dark hair.

"I'm sorry?" Billie said.

"Not as sorry as that blighter is." The woman pointed at the cracked shell of the marine creature at Billie's feet. She laughed. "I was saying that what you're looking at is roe."

Billie glanced at the creature. "You mean the dark stuff? Is it like caviar?"

"No. The yellow lobes. They're a delicacy. They're actually the gonads."

Billie tasted bile again. She rose shakily.

"You all right?" the woman said.

"Yes. Yes. A bit faint."

"Guilt, is it?"

Billie's head jerked up. For some reason, she thought of Antony. On her mental to-do list, the one that varied from the official list that Antony drew up each day, was the agenda item *Let Antony down gently.*

"What do you mean?" she said.

The woman shrugged her large shoulders and pulled down her hood to reveal a rotund face with several echoes of chins. The hair on her head was sparse and coarse, and there were additional dark hairs on her chin and one sprouting from a mole on her cheek.

"You broke a heart," the woman said.

Billie stared.

The woman pointed at the sea creature. "That's a heart urchin."

"Oh. I—" Billie didn't know how to respond. "Are there local tales about them?"

"Undoubtedly. You're probably cursed now."

When the woman barked a sharp laugh, Billie gasped with relief.

"I'm June," the woman said.

"Billie."

"Daft name for a pretty thing."

Ordinarily, Billie might have rankled. But she only smiled at the compliment.

"And that's Pressburger," Billie said, turning and pointing.

But Pressburger wasn't there.

"Your dog? He'll have wandered to the cave. It's half a mile that way. Full of interesting scents, no doubt."

"Thanks. Well, then, I should…" Billie gestured along the beach.

"I'll come with you."

"You really needn't."

"All the same, I will."

They plodded towards the headland. It was slow going, as Billie's boots kept sinking and it took effort to pull them free. She glanced at June's feet. Though June was wearing only lime-green Crocs (hints of ragged yellow toenails visible through the holes), and though she was twice Billie's size, she seemed to have no problem navigating the soft surface.

"You live here, I suppose?" Billie asked.

"Indeed."

"Have you always?" It was impossible to imagine June in a city, a supermarket, anywhere but here.

"Feels like it. What brings you here?"

"I needed to walk my dog."

"Nope."

Billie stumbled slightly. "I'm sorry?"

"That's not it."

Billie recovered herself and smiled. She was used to guarding her identity and her purpose, for fear of making waves. But it could do no harm to speak freely to this woman. In all likelihood she was a hermit who didn't talk to anyone else, even within the village.

"I'm a location scout," Billie said.

"Ah."

"For films and TV shows."

"I see."

"I search around for the right location to fit the requirements of a script."

June nodded, then looked around at the beach, the rocky cliffs, the sea. "And this place?"

"I hoped it might be suitable for a film I'm working on. It's about a painter who sets up a studio in a fishing village, then develops a bond with a local fisherwoman. But it's set in 1905, when the village and its businesses would have been thriving."

"You don't think my village would do."

June's flat tone was difficult to interpret. Billie could impose onto it accusation or hopefulness or boredom.

"Other villages might suit my needs with less adjustment," she said diplomatically. "And the beach is stonier than I'd hoped."

"Pick 'em up, then," June said.

Billie stopped walking and looked down at the pebbles at her feet. They weren't large. Possibly, they could be removed, and then the beach would be a great deal more attractive. She bent and picked up a couple of pebbles. They were sea-smoothed and pleasant to rub her thumb against.

Registering that June was watching her closely, she slipped the pebbles into her pocket. Then she feared that June would accuse her of theft, a crime to add to the murder of the heart urchin.

June only shook her head and continued walking.

Billie trailed behind her. She was distracted by a collection of objects nestled at the foot of the cliffs. Two towels lay on the ground, one weighted down at the corners with rocks, the other free of two of its anchors and flapping in the breeze. Beside them was a hard plastic coolbox and a single pair of red sandals.

Billie turned to scan the area. She could see nobody.

She hurried to catch up with June. The beach became a narrow strip that led around the outcrop. Now Billie saw the cave. The outcrop was little more than a shell around this vast empty space, like the mouth of a whale directed seaward to catch prey.

"Pressburger!" she called.

Her voice echoed brightly, as if she were shouting in a cathedral.

"Press!"

A faint bark came from the dark depths. Billie's shoulders slumped in relief.

"The script does actually include a cave," she said to June as she waited for her dog. "At one point the painter encounters a local smuggler. As you can imagine, the smuggler's already embroiled with the fisherwoman would-be lover…"

She trailed off. June wouldn't care about any of this.

"What would it involve?" June asked.

"Involve? Oh, you mean if I chose this area for filming. There'd be a film crew, but nothing major. We're talking BFI-backed indie, not Hollywood glitz. Still, I'd hope for Romola Garai, say, if not Kate Winslet. Not that casting is anything to do with me, but I do have a sense for a project with momentum."

"People. Bustling around. Energy."

"Yes. But not for long. No more than three weeks, for outdoor scenes. Then the talent would leave and the crew would hang around a few days for establishing shots and soundbeds. Interiors would all be in the studio."

"How many people?"

Billie weighed up whether to lie, but June's manner demanded the truth. "Fifty, minimum. Probably closer to sixty or seventy."

June looked out to sea.

Billie went on, "Any locals inconvenienced would be remunerated. Anyone whose property is used could earn real money. And then there's the boost to tourism, after release. *That* can bring new energy to a place, I promise you." She almost added her usual suggestion that locals might find themselves onscreen as background extras. But no director would allow somebody as ugly as June into frame.

Pressburger barked again. Why hadn't he come to her?

Billie made her way into the dark. It took her a long while to locate Pressburger in the gloom, despite his frequent outbursts.

He was at the rear of the cave, his front paws upon a bright orange raincoat that had been abandoned there. When Billie tried to pull him away, he returned the spot and barked again. He was preoccupied with the wall of the cave. Billie saw a shadow there. No, not a shadow, a sort of stain. She reached out and touched it, fearing it might be blood. But no, it was a dark residue, thick like tar, but not tacky. Embedded within it were small, hard globules that reminded her of caviar.

Pressburger barked again, then lunged toward the wall and licked it.

"No!" Billie cried, aghast. "Come *on*, Pressburger." She affixed his lead to his collar and dragged him away.

Her first impression as she left the cave was that her eyes had refused to adjust. Then she realised that it was simply that dusk had fallen. She hadn't looked at her watch the entire time she had been at the village. She must have arrived far later than she had supposed.

"You'll be hungry," June said.

"No, I don't think so," Billie replied distantly. Then her stomach growled. "Maybe a little."

"To the pub!" June said.

They set off without further discussion.

June set down two pints of black stout on the round table. Billie's stomach turned.

"Thank you," she said, and smiled.

Pressburger was sprawled on the floorboards at June's feet. Billie had only ever seen him so comfortable in an unfamiliar location if there was a roaring fire. But there was no fire in the small front room of the pub. In fact, it was icy cold, and Billie hadn't even dared take off her puffer jacket.

"You're sure he's okay there?" she asked.

"The others do seem to prefer the yard," June said, gesturing at a grimy window.

Billie peered through the window to see a paved terrace. Directly beyond it, tall waves hurled themselves from the sea to crash against a stone jetty. On the terrace, three picnic benches had been pushed to one side. The reclaimed space was filled with static blotches that were difficult to make out in the deepening dusk. Six or seven dogs, all lying prone like Pressburger.

Billie shuddered.

"But your dog can stay in here, just this once," June concluded.

"There'll only be the once," Billie said quickly. "I must be getting back, as soon as I've eaten."

"It's a long way."

Billie frowned. "I haven't told you where I'm going."

"Far away. The people you'll bring, they'll be nothing like the people here."

"They're professionals."

June responded with a low hum.

"People came here from far away in the past," Billie said. "Artists, drawn to the village because of its landscape. The sea. That's why my assistant put your village on my list of places to visit. Because that's the subject of the film, too, you see. An artist called Pieter Lennox comes from a distant location – Manchester – and rents a home, intending to study the area and to paint seascapes. But then he befriends Sylvie Gray, a humble fisherman's daughter, and she teaches him what's *in* the sea. The life within. Then Lennox becomes far more enamoured with that aspect than seascape watercolours, and he begins to specialise. And, of course, he falls head over heels for Sylvie."

"What's in the sea," June repeated in an undertone.

"That's right. Crustaceans, like that strange thing I found on the beach." Abruptly, Billie felt she might be sick. She thought of the dark insides of the heart urchin. Though she wanted to wash away the iron taste on her tongue, she couldn't bring herself to drink the stout. Perhaps she could talk away her nausea. "Lennox was a real painter. Sylvie was real, too. But this all happened down in Dorset. I'm not looking at Dorset locations because it's been a nightmare getting permissions down there ever since *Broadchurch*. It's better up here in the north-east. Quieter."

"The life within," June echoed.

Billie had overestimated the woman's intelligence. She unzipped her rucksack and pulled out a slim hardback book titled *Pieter Lennox: The Embrace of the Waves*. "Look," she said, opening it at a random page to reveal detailed illustrations of sea snails, the whorls of their shells immaculate. Anybody might mistake them for photographs. "This is the sort of thing that preoccupied him."

June shuffled from her stool to sit beside Billie on the threadbare velveteen bench. She smelled of brine. She reached across Billie to turn the pages of the book.

"Good," she said. "Yes, very good."

She kept turning pages, then stopped and tapped a thick finger on a diagram with the label *Spatangoida*. The main picture showed something that looked rather like a hairy potato, but the illustration alongside showed it without its brushlike covering: it was the same type of urchin Billie had accidentally destroyed on the beach.

"I really didn't mean to—" Billie began.

"Who the fuck cares," June spat.

Billie froze. June turned overleaf and sighed contentedly.

This page depicted another type of sea urchin. It was shaped like a globe – a true globe, slightly flattened at the poles – and covered with thick spines like porcupine quills.

"Beautiful," June said.

The creature was anything but beautiful. It looked rather like June herself: bloated and riddled with spikes.

"Clever, too," June added. "Do you know how sea urchins operate?"

"You mean how they move?"

"They walk on hundreds of tiny feet, so they barely seem to touch the sea bed. But I meant how they live. Survive. Thrive."

"Tell me," Billie said.

"They feed on algae. Kelp. The detritus of the sea. Invertebrates, too, when I can get 'em, but that's not often, because sea urchins are lethargic. Lazy. Their preferred method of feeding is to find a suitable location full of kelp, then scrape away the algae over time. Their jaws are known as Aristotle's lantern, did you know that? It was the five-sided shape that gave old Aristotle the idea." She raised a fat hand and made pincer movements with all four of her fingers and her thumb. Then she moved her hand so that it hovered over a sugar bowl on the table, and she continued the same motions as she lowered it, digging into the congealed grains of sugar. She said, "There's an additional benefit to this lackadaisical method of feeding: it gradually creates a depression in the surface, forming a safe hideaway for the urchin."

Billie stared at June's digits half-buried in the sugar. The old woman's enthusiasm for the subject of sea urchins struck her as unnatural. And then there was her odd insertion of the phrase *when I can get 'em.*

"You'll go," June said in close to a whisper, "and you'll tell your people about this place. They'll come here in droves." She raised her glass of stout and slurped from its head, then licked her lips sensually.

Billie studied her. Up close, June's coarse hair was even more offensive. Each root on her hair occupied its own distinct territory. The effect was more like the thick spines of a hedgehog than normal hair.

"I still can't tell whether you're dismayed, or whether you quite like the idea of us filming here," Billie said.

"Drink," June said.

Billie took a sip, just to be polite. The stout was incredibly bitter, but it did ease the grumbling of her stomach a little, before it sank like a stone.

"They should come," June said. "Bring life to this place." Another sip, more froth, another lick of the lips. "You see, it can't last. Once the kelp is gone, what's left is called an urchin barren. A wasteland. No life, no food."

Now Billie understood that June had been attempting a parable of sorts.

She managed a faint chuckle. "It does seem a little barren here. A little dead."

June's eyes flicked up.

"Of course, it's out of season," Billie said hurriedly, "Nobody'd expect it to be thronging right now. But I saw the state of the buildings. It looks like even the Airbnb properties haven't been used in some time. And, well, I haven't seen a soul apart from you."

A smile formed slowly on June's face.

"What about Sam?" she said.

"I'm sorry, who's—"

A shadow fell upon the table. A man stood before them, carrying two bowls.

"This is Sam," June said. "Say hello, Sam."

"Hello," the man said. His voice was strained, as though he were unused to speaking. His pale face suggested he didn't see the sun much, and his gauntness spoke of illness.

He deposited the bowls unsteadily, sloshing liquid onto the surface of the table, then dabbing at the spill ineffectively with his fingertips.

"All right, Sam," June said. "You can go."

Billie gazed at the contents of her bowl. The broth had no colour, only a slightly opaque sheen. Suspended in it were strings of dull green vegetable matter.

"What is this?" she breathed.

"Seaweed."

"Is it a local delicacy?"

June laughed. "It's all there is."

Billie's stomach groaned again. But she couldn't bring herself to try the broth.

"Don't make me eat it," she pleaded.

June watched her closely, then said, "All right. I won't." She took up a spoon and began to sup broth from her bowl. "Now. Are we agreed? You'll go back, then you'll bring your people here."

Billie thought not of production crews but of Antony. She shook her head. "I'm sorry to disappoint, but on reflection your village simply isn't suitable. The buildings would take enormous work to convince as functional fishermen's cottages. The beach is very plain and, well, not an *eyesore*, but, you know…" She coughed nervously. "I'd hoped the cove might suit as a smuggler's base, but it's too big – in widescreen you'd never be able to get a sense of the shape of its mouth."

She remembered the dark stain above the orange raincoat, and Pressburger's frantic response, and she stifled the impulse to add that the cave had struck her as, for want of a better word, *haunted*.

June said, "But you could choose this place, all the same."

Billie hesitated. "Yes, I could. But it'd require an enormous amount of work. More craftspeople to make the buildings match the era, more time taken."

June nodded slowly.

"It's tempting," she said.

"Yes, I'm tempted."

Why had she said that? There must be dozens of villages on the north-eastern coast that would be better suited.

"You're just one person." June raised her glass and gulped stout. Froth remained on her upper lip. The contrast between the beige bubbles and her coarse hairs was obscene. "All those additional people… yes, that would be more satisfactory than just you."

"What do you mean by that?" Billie asked.

June ignored the question. "You should consider your decision overnight."

"No. I must get back this evening."

"It's far too late for that."

Billie glanced out of the small window. It was black dark. The dogs on the terrace were invisible now. The waves were only shadows rising and creeping to land.

"How could it—"

"Enough," June said. "Rest, and consider your decision. Let it sink in."

Almost involuntarily, Billie rose from her seat. She nudged Pressburger with her foot. He didn't stir.

"You can leave him here," June said.

"I could never do that."

"Try to take him. But he'll not move."

It was true.

She had slept far better than expected, despite the wind hissing through the gap beneath the window sash, despite the bed being slightly angled due to rotten, subsiding floorboards. Last night Billie had been surprised when Sam had led her not to a room within the pub, but to one of the local buildings. Like the one she had glimpsed earlier in the day, it had clearly been kitted out as a holiday let in recent years, which made it difficult to understand how it had fallen into such disarray so quickly. The windows were clouded with greenish stains, and the sitting-room sofa was suffused with some viscous substance that must have been carried on the sea air.

Energised, she swung her arms as she emerged from the narrow lane to the sea front. The sea was far calmer this morning, a flat basin below a clear almond-coloured sky, and the tide was in, eliminating the beach. Billie thought of the towels she had seen yesterday, the coolbox, the sandals, and wondered if they had been washed away.

What did it matter? The day was beautiful and she was happy.

She turned to the pub. Its wooden sign hung flaccidly. It bore no name, but on the sign was an illustration of an old-fashioned lantern, the sort she could imagine held aloft by a smuggler operating at night.

As before, several dogs lay on the terrace. It didn't strike Billie as unusual now that it was daylight and the wind had died.

Pressburger was amongst them. He didn't stir when she called his name.

She couldn't blame him. It was glorious here. The appeal of staying put and relishing the calm was impossible to dismiss.

She went inside the pub. Sam stood behind the bar, staring blankly out of the window.

"Where can I find June?" Billie asked. She was surprised at the enthusiasm in her voice. She *did* need to find June, as soon as possible, but the reason escaped her. Perhaps she simply needed to say goodbye.

Sam pointed through the window, at the outcrop further along the coast.

Billie's voice cracked as she said, "But the tide is in. How can I reach her?"

Sam didn't reply.

Billie left the building. On the terrace she muttered, "Let sleeping dogs lie," and then hurried to the stone jetty.

She hesitated only for a moment on the stone steps that ended at the frothing surface of the seawater. She gasped in delight as the water sloshed halfway up her calves. Though it was cold at first, after a few seconds the water swilling in her boots had warmed nicely.

She strode in the direction of the outcrop. Soon she was jogging, sending up spray with each step.

"June!" she cried. "June!"

She stopped at the mouth of the cave. This morning its interior was visible, illuminated by sepia sunlight. A bent figure was at the rear of the cave. It was June in her dull brown poncho. She was crouching before the rear wall. Her tongue was pressed against it, making short, sharp motions as though scraping it clean.

Billie turned to look at the flat, featureless sea.

She released a long exhalation.

Yes, this location was perfect.

Something Peculiar

from

Guy Adams

Holly Black

Sarah Brooks

Emma Coleman

Timothy J. Jarvis

John Langan

Tim Major

Alexander Milne

Mark Morris

Danie Ware

Marian Womack

The Way Through the Woods

"...the sea awaits..."

—*Introduction*—

THE JOURNEY had been mostly uneventful. At one point her son had taken the baby in his arms, although she weighed maybe a full quarter of what he did, and carried her out into the interconnecting train carriages. Her stomach had contracted slightly. She could imagine all sorts of horrors – an automatic door opening by accident, a fall. But she did not want to interfere with their carefully curated mood: her son seemed, if not happy, at least accepting of the trip. And Eric loved his baby sister: whatever happened, whatever was happening, she held onto this one fact. Her knee had not bothered her the whole journey so far, which must be a good sign.

The island turned out to be both exactly what she had expected and somehow different, which made her oddly uneasy about how the days would unfold. If she was going to get her work done, she needed every member of her family happy. There were some woods, and Eric had wanted woods, had insisted on it. He wanted to go to some woods. She had asked why.

'To get lost in them,' he had replied, and Mark had laughed. But the exchange had made her oddly unsettled.

She had started listing them, extolling their number, reading the names aloud: Glecknabae, Cnocnicol, Torr. Gaelic names that she didn't know how to pronounce. She made an effort, tried to convey some enthusiasm. She was pretending, of course: she had no intention of visiting those places, and would not allow the child to dictate the terms of the trip. They were first and foremost going for her sake, so she could find some inspiration, finish the songs that had been eluding her. Have a full album of material. Enact her great return. Lure back her so-called career. All the damn shenanigans. Everything would be fine then, she thought; everything would return where it was meant to be. She wouldn't need to work at all hours anymore; she wouldn't miss any family moments. At some point Mark had complained that thank God she was almost done with the bloody album, because composing those few songs had almost 'wrecked their family life'. And she was really trying, trying to rush to the finish line. But it wasn't happening; and so the record company had suggested the trip. As she was still breastfeeding and Anna was too little, the baby had to come with her. And if Anna had to come, Mark had to come to look after her. And leaving Eric alone with relatives he hardly knew was insensitive and cruel: they would all have to come.

This was it, now or never. She had to get it done. Mark would be proud, and she would feel like her true self again. This trip was for her, and she was thankful. She needed space to work, inspiration; but also a break, or so she kept repeating to herself, trying not to feel too guilty; a break, given the baby and the unsuccessful attempts to write something meaningful so soon after giving birth, and absolutely everything else that she had put herself through during the last year and a half. She imagined that Mark had only agreed to it all out of fear: she could see it in his eyes; he was waiting for something, she wasn't sure what.

At least they hadn't had to move a finger. The record company had presented them with the facts: they would take such and such a train, and would stay in this house, where the fridge would be full, and the music room well-equipped; and they would be back on this date. Nothing was expected of him, not even thinking about where they would go and what they would do: all he needed was to tag along, help with the kids, allow her a modicum of space. Two songs wasn't much, was it? But she knew he was oddly resentful, resentful of precisely this, the fact that nothing was expected from him. As was his habit, he had packed a bag with as many books as he could possibly carry: reading as a protection, reading as a shield, reading book after book after book as a manner of interacting with her as little as possible. She imagined most poets were like that: she hoped, secretly, that most poets were like that. This gave her a vague reason not to get cross, accept it as a personality trait, to know herself defeated and accept this defeat. She evaded acknowledging something else, that he also used the children as a shield from her, of course he did.

—Verse—

They decided to walk from the ferry to the house the record company had rented, although she was wary of Mark's insistence that it was only ten minutes' walk. Ten minutes' walk for Mark always ended up being twenty for her, and her knee was already throbbing. It would be difficult to handle the bags and hold Eric's hand. She longed so much to submerge herself in some water, any water would do.

Ever since pain had arrived in her life, she had been happiest hiding in perilously full baths, or swimming in the town's lido – the longest lido ever built – or, on the few occasions when she had been able to escape, floating in the ocean.

The scales had arrived later, almost as an afterthought. At first she had failed to notice them, or at least she had not paid any attention to her knee while it didn't bother her. But then the itching had started, one evening, over dinner. Covered by the baby blankets, and the bundle that was baby Anna herself, mercilessly suck-sucking, she had not been able to pay much attention to it. And then she had fallen asleep, and only the next morning she had a chance to check what was what. She woke up covered in so much sweat that she thought she was still diving in the imagined sea of her dream.

There were little flakes coming away from under her knee. It was not clear what it was, perhaps some kind of eczema. She did not remember what had happened all those years back, when she had breastfed Eric, but assumed that whatever it was would resolve itself. She was too tired to do anything about it. And she still had two whole songs to write.

On the island, she grabbed Eric's hand to cross the road, although he didn't want to, of course; but he was still little, and there were roads to cross and cars to avoid, and she wasn't going to let him have his way. They marched on, Mark pushing the baby chair. After a moment Eric accepted the hand that was offered, and seemed happy with what he was seeing. She smiled to herself, held onto the moment.

He wasn't a bad child, not really, or at least she did not imagine him as worse than other seven-year-olds. But she did not recognise him in the communications that came to her and Mark from the school. They had tried to rationalise it: children that age sometimes started to play more forcibly than before. It was only normal: part of the process of growing up. But the concept of the 'kill list' had worried her, as much as it had scared some of his classmates. They had tried to discuss where the idea had come from. Could it be from some of the cartoons he watched? Would they need perhaps to supervise those more closely? Mark was right, it was an odd turning-point age, and perhaps he had been exposed to a more violent kind of animation, suitable for older children. They'd had a chat with Eric, and his tablet was confiscated for a while: from now on, he would watch his series with her on the family TV. He didn't seem to mind. But even that was too much, a new duty to add to all her other duties. She was being selfish, she knew that. Wasn't parenting exactly about doing things like this? But, with each new duty, a portion of her dwindling day was again out of her control, and she was becoming exhausted by the process of cutting off bits of herself, limb by limb; knocked out by seeing her days as a succession of unending to-dos. Everything conspired to overwhelm her, like a blanket covering her with tasks and lists that she never seemed to finish. The truth was that she hadn't written a really good song in years, and her last mediocre attempts had happened already months ago aeons away.

—*Chorus*—

This anxiety had given way to the dreams. She was in the water, in the middle of a deep chasm – the brim of an abyss – floating in the cold, dark liquid. She wasn't sure, but she thought she had a tail.

There were other dreams, but these came during her waking hours. She had dreamed of going away by herself, of course she had, only to feel the known anxiety, to realise that she needed them around her. And so, she had selfishly dragged them all to the island. Mark claimed he did not mind, but she could see he was worried. For the first few months of the new baby her head had been too cloudy to compose anything good, but she had said to herself *it will pass, it will pass*. The 'non-writing' had persisted, and now it seemed here to stay. How disgustingly selfish she was… She checked her notes: the chorus. She had not been able to settle on that at all.

'Lucy, dear. Lucy?'

Mark was talking to her, and she managed a weak smile. Yes, of course, the island is as beautiful as they'd hoped it would be, he reassured the owner of the house, who had been instructed by the record company to cook that first supper. She jerked herself into life: she had been worrying about the song. How could she? She looked at her children, they were reassuringly beautiful. Everyone looked in good spirits. The walk up the promenade had been breathtaking, with a deep green sea framed by mountains, so many that it had been difficult to understand looking back where the ferry had come from. She had read the guide thoroughly before the trip, and knew to expect a museum, gothic ruined churches, an imposing stately home, endless fields, standing stones, Neolithic cairns, white one-storey cottages, beaches, and always, from almost any road, a sea view, sometimes with another island in the distance, or a mountain rising. Palm trees, ferry daytrips, and even pictures of a sunny mini golf, were also present, elements more suited to a southern resort, thanks to the miraculous micro-climate. She cheerfully declared to the woman that the island had something for everybody. She did not mention how she secretly dreaded how they would cope without her if she needed to stay behind to write. She was going to join them for some outings, of course; but she needed to work. She always needed to work.

'I want woods,' Eric had said. 'I want woods on our holiday.'

'Woods? Whatever for?'

'To get lost in them.'

Mark's laughter, her constant worry. She showed him the guide, again: there were woods on the island. She started reading their names out loud to him, again. Would he see how she made an effort for him? Under her knee, around it, and over it, the scales were again itching, bothering her.

There were meant to be seals, but they seemed to have decided not to show up. They had decided on a schedule, and it seemed that this was the only day when they could make it to Scalpsie Bay. She felt more disappointed than she had expected. What had she thought: that the seals would just wait around for her to come? She knew it was silly, but she had secretly hoped for some kind of revelation, a *moment*, a way to feel something again that perhaps she could have treasured, an image she could use in the lyrics she was working on, or at least put away in a notebook for future use. The chorus... she had nothing yet. Mark had started talking feverishly by now, trying to improvise ways to save the day, but for whom? Eric had only agreed on the promise of going to some woods the following morning. And then she realised he was trying to save the day from her.

She didn't know until that exact moment how much he feared her and her reactions; she felt strangely cold in the face of the knowledge. She reassured him with a smile, went back to her notebook, while Mark and Eric entertained the baby with sandcastles and moats, and woods made of seaweed.

Time is slow, life is fast
The petals of the clock
Decay
And years become minutes...

It was going to be a ballad. She had been told not to write another ballad. But she couldn't help it. What did they know: her agent, her producer, even Mark?

And there she was again, floating over the abyss, in the middle of the deep, deep water.

It was all an impossible dream, she knew, she knew... But it felt so real.

She woke up with a jerk. She had dozed on her chair in the sand. Her family wasn't anywhere, and she panicked for a minute. She got up in a flash, looked around... They were there, walking towards her. Everything was fine, everything was fine... They were all fine.

Time will find you
Will destroy you...
Fragments of the world
Surround you everywhere...

She inspected the tourist map that the house owner had left for them on the kitchen counter. It was a crude drawing of the island, punctuated here and there by images of peregrine falcons and merlins and hen harriers and skylarks and golden eagles, indicating where best to see them, and red deer and roe deer, and otters, and the seals they had now missed. So far they had only seen oystercatchers by the bucketload, and she imagined the rest of the animals were hidden somewhere. It was an island, but she could not see any indication of which kind of marine animals they could see. This was surprising. Also, why did she want to see fish?

Perhaps because her dream the previous night had been so vivid. She was under the surface, trying to hide in the deep. Through the crystalline surface, she could see Mark, and Eric, and even baby Anna, in a little paddle boat, fishing rods out, and she knew they had been trying to get her, and that the only way to escape was by diving deeper. Deeper and deeper...

As they were at the southern end of the island, she suggested a walk between the ruined gothic chapel and one of the stone circles.

'We can catch ghosts!' she said to Eric animatedly. Ghost hunting was one of his latest games.

'Okay.'

They had only been able to dip their toes, the water was so cold. It was almost a painful effort, to turn her back to the water, to deny herself what she truly wanted.

Mark dutifully put the baby back in the baby car seat, and they went in. They drove among the green fields punctuated here and there by sheep, and sudden views of the sea, sometimes to the left of the car, sometimes to the right, reminding her of how small the island really was, especially on the southern peninsula. The sea was calling… and she was ignoring it. And after each turn, there it was again. Her knee was throbbing in pain; the itching ensued.

At some point, at their left, they had got a glimpse of what looked like a small woodland, and she thought from her memory of the map it ought to be Torr Wood. They came into the carpark and walked towards the ruin. On one side, there was a small graveyard, and Eric decided to stay there. She did not manage to encourage him to see the interior of the ruin. She had hoped to instil in him a sense of adventure into the unknown, but she had obviously not succeeded. There were farms around the chapel, and the place, even with its gothic sensibilities, failed to be anything but wholesome in the sun. For something to do, she checked the guide. There was something close enough, a small loch, Loch na Leighe, which the guide informed her was Gaelic for 'Healing Lake.' *The origins of the name are a mystery.* She was obscurely curious about the effect it would have on her son to encourage him to have a dip there. Would he be cured of his sudden, unexpected morbidity? He had been such a sweet child; nothing spookier than Scooby Doo. No, she repeated to herself. He was still sweet. There was nothing at all wrong with him.

The baby protested from the chair, and she went mechanically to grab her, and found a place to sit and feed her on a stone. She looked around for Mark. He was leaning against a rock, checking his mobile. His slight smile made her think he must be on X, and that he had recently written something extremely witty, and was getting a good response. She felt her insides burning. Not far away from Mark, Eric was kicking some stones, obviously bored and unattended. Why didn't her husband occupy himself more with his son? Would he dream of 'kill lists' if Mark put a few more hours in? And what about her? Wasn't she also responsible?

She tried to remember the lyrics she had been working on back at the beach, conjure up the melody... Nothing. She knew she had taken copious notes but was suddenly resentful: this was 'baby brain', foggy brain; it would be worse during the menopause. When could a woman *do* these things, for god's sake?

Now she tended to the baby. Why on earth couldn't Mark see that she was doing this, and make sure Eric got the same attention from the other available adult? No wonder their sweet son was feeling displaced by the whole new family dynamic, and was developing new and upsetting patterns of behaviour. Morosely she knew that talking to Mark would be useless.

It was so silent that she could hear the clicking of insects. She thought vaguely of Mark, of his capacity of being absent even when he was there with them. Was he going to leave her? Would it then be easier if she left him first? She considered this, but she knew it would be impossible for her to make the first move. It would require an amount of energy she did not possess.

The petals on your grave
By the ruined church
It could not last... Oh no, baby, it couldn't...

Her knee was itching, her brain was itching. She wished... She wished for... She knew what she wished for: a big expanse of water, and being alone in it. Diving deep.

Why did she want that? Wasn't her family enough? Weren't Mark, Eric, Anna, enough? Why not find a wood for Eric, walk all the way through it with him, from beginning to end, holding his hand? Make him happy? Because she knew, obscurely, that it was his wishes or her wishes; it could not be both.

As they left the ruins and drove to another little beach, she saw it from the car window: something so shiny and unexpected, coming up for breath from out of the water. Half fish, half *something else*, and, in case there was any doubt, with a beautiful pair of blue eyes.

The lady at the café had been so kind, coming to her rescue. Eric had been impossible, loudly complaining over breakfast that he wanted his woods. She had timidly intervened, suggesting a walk in the Moss Wood. Now, moss was something Lucy could understand, get behind.

—Chorus—

The small car park was well signposted, and they promptly found themselves in a fairyland of broadleaf woodland, a calm green and brown sea, resting under the blue skies. The sunbeams played around the leaves and the branches, forming little patterns of shade. Anna gurgled happily in her BabyBjörn, and Eric, and even Mark, seemed contented. They almost failed to find the circular path, and wandered without direction, there was little sense of getting lost among the cheerful, anaemic birches.

Eric had gone ahead, faster than she had thought possible. Where was he?

'Mark! Where's he gone?'

'There's a viewpoint, remember? With a bench. The B&B lady mentioned it.'

'You think that's where he's gone?'

'Where else? He's probably bored and wants to sit down and sulk already. Anyway, no one can get lost on a path like this.'

'Yes, but what if he's gone off the path, Mark?' Why did she sound like this? Why did she always sound like she was scolding, when she was really worried, scared?

'Relax! This place is tiny, he can't disappear.'

But she doubted it. She went ahead at pace, leaving Mark and the baby behind, her heart throbbing.

Eric was sitting by the viewpoint, exactly as Mark had indicated that he would be.

It came to her then, in a flash, the whole chorus:

Take me there, through the woods
Take me the way through the woods
Don't get lost
The sea awaits…

—Bridge—

It had probably been one of the famous Scalpsie Bay seals, lost and in the wrong area of the island. It had probably been a trick of the light. She kept repeating this to herself.

But she kept thinking about it, all the same. She was also wondering whether she could pre-empt what was always going to happen by getting there first. She considered her options. Years ago, when she had been looking after a small Eric, she had felt exhausted in that way for the first time, in that way in which resting did not make any difference to her energy levels, her knee had beginning to throb even if she did not walk anywhere. Endless x-rays would follow, never finding anything. On her worst days, she had started to fantasise strongly with leaving everything behind to go and live in a caravan. She had been so close to giving up. The only reason why she hadn't done so was Eric. She loved Mark, or at least she imagined that she did. But he did not understand what she was going through. To see her body shutting down like that, while she still considered herself a young woman. To start having all those limitations, to understand, little by little, that this would be her life from now on, a slow declining curve.

Everything had begun to lose its form. First, she had to abandon some of the touring work she had picked up in the folk circuit. But that was alright: she could still write her songs and record them from the privacy of her home. Then, soon after, she had had to accept that she simply could not sit on the floor to play with her son, as she might not be able to get up afterwards. This knowledge had crept up on her, seemingly out of nowhere. And these little things were the worst. What kind of person was she now, if she could not do her work, which until then had defined her? What kind of mother was she, if she could not play with her son? The world itself was losing its form, had become shapeless, nebulous. She was looking for patterns now, in Mark's behaviour, in Eric's behaviour. But she also saw other signs.

She now knew the island was sending her signs too. And it was saying that it wasn't them, that it had never been them. It was her. She would never write another song, another *good* song. She would try, she would fail. She would return with her mediocre song, and the album would be shelved. And that would be the end. The real end. Of absolutely everything.

—Verse—

The selkie had not really been there. Or perhaps it had been one of those wild swimmers who were everywhere these days. She thought the term itself was funny. Where she came from, swimming was easily available. Boring, in fact. Here, a lot of time and effort had to be put into the activity, she supposed, from finding appropriate places, to accessing the water in the rugged coasts or steep riverbanks; and then you had to deal with the cold, or the pollution. It must have been a woman, wearing a special kind of swimming costume she had never seen before, like those expensive balloon-shaped after-swim coats preferred by the people in the know. Her eyes had tricked her. She put it down to stress, lack of sleep. The baby was rejecting bottles altogether, so she found herself back at breastfeeding on demand again. This was not the way things were meant to be going, but Lucy had no idea how to wean her. She had breastfed Eric on demand until he was two and a half, but she had been much younger, had more energy. When she had needed to go on a little tour, she had left him with her mother, and when she got back that was that, solid foods only. It would now be difficult to encourage a similar routine. Her mother was much older now, and refused point blank to help them. She felt worthless, stupid. But why? She was an adult, with a successful career – at least until now – a family of her own, a dutifully-paid mortgage. She was, by all accounts, a successful grown up. She tried to put the notion out of her head. She tried very hard and almost succeeded. She got up and walked to the window, moved the curtain an inch to enjoy the view. She did not want to wake everybody up. There were other notions that assaulted her sometimes, memories she knew vaguely she would have to deal with someday. The distressed face of Eric as a toddler, when things were sad or worrying, or he simply did not understand them. She had probably been shouting at Mark again, probably about something minor, and would feel awful afterwards. Her lying to the paediatrician about Anna's weight. Why had she done such a thing? She had been worried she would be labelled a bad mother. And, anyway, things were resolving themselves. The baby looked better now and would do so for as long as she could drink her milk. She would have to make an effort and continue to feed her. There was no need to believe that there could be a pattern emerging, that the baby would stop gaining weight, or would do so at a slower rate than was necessary.

She looked at them, at her family, placidly sleeping. She did not really know Mark now: she had lost him somehow, that much she could admit to herself. And her son, who had been such a lovely companion once, would also grow into a stranger, a grown man with whom she would have nothing in common, nothing to share. A whole separate being from herself, who would not need her any longer. The notion was outlandish. But maybe he was a stranger, even now. He looked so peaceful but also so different from how he normally looked during the day, as if he had been changed over by the fairies in his sleep, stolen away, another boy left in his place, a boy perhaps made of wood, or of sand, or of dreams, a boy who might break if she touched him. She would have to be so careful to keep him safe, to keep this new boy out of trouble. She remembered a man she had seen on a television programme: after he and his wife had been injured in a car crash, he was convinced that his real wife had been killed in the accident, and that the woman now living with him was some sort of substitute, a fake. He called her Wife Two, could not bear to touch her, hardly communicated with her. He had some sort of strange mental illness, Capgras syndrome. Funny to think of that now.

It wasn't only she who was fragile; it was the whole world that had turned insecure. When had it happened, exactly? She realised how precarious their existence really was, how they were only ever one or two paychecks from total disaster. If something were to happen, they might lose everything. And she knew that they were also acclimatised to this, their own normality, so much so that they lived outside of fear somehow, not thinking about this possibility, when a mishap would destroy the carefully crafted life that they had conjured up, and that she at this moment knew to be a mirage, looking out to sea and mountains across the Firth of Clyde. They were being careful, she knew, also with each other. But one day it could all abruptly end. And then, there was yet another fear, even more unthinkable, the fear that something horrible would happen to them, something far more disturbing than failing to pay the council tax. Something truly horrendous, unspeakable. And she knew, instantly, that they would not survive it. They couldn't. And that thought revealed to her in an instant the true fragility of the life they had built, starting with her marriage: it would only take one second, one single event, for it to come crashing down. She looked at her notebook abandoned at her side of the bed, with her careful notes for a song in two different coloured inks, black and red. Would she bother to do any of that, if the worst happened? Would she even write another song? She realised, suddenly, how much was weighing on this one song that, try as she might, was not coming. And she wondered if she had indeed tempted fate by trying to write, if she was somehow betraying her children, if they were going to suffer because she was not ready when the time came, because she did not remember that what she had to do was to think. Observe. Plan. Find water. Find shelter. Would she ever need to find shelter for them? Or would she be writing colour-coded notes instead, lyrics and melodies that sounded ten times better in her head than she could ever make them in reality?

She had never realised, not fully, not truly until this very moment, how unsafe her situation was. She wanted to scream. Nothing is solid. Nothing at all. She knew this now.

She looked at her family, and could see only shadows.

—Post-chorus, or end—

The water was cold, but it was lovely to be doing something for herself. From the sea she could see the two windows of the beautifully-furnished attic where the bedroom was. Her family was there.

First, the seals appeared, then the selkie. She could not know if it was the same one, but thought it was. With a lucidity that surprised even her, or was perhaps communicated directly into her brain somehow, she understood: the woman had fallen into the water and given herself up to it. There was peace in the thought that whatever happened there was always that possibility. In the twilight, she could be a seal, or a woman, or, at times, the two. Lucy wondered, not a shape-shifter herself, how long her human breath would last, to transport her deep below the sea.

She wanted to ask the woman, why did you choose this? *How* did you choose this?

And she recognised her face on the creature's face, and looked down: the scales now covered her whole leg, no longer itching.

The Way Through the Woods

> *Time is slow, life is fast*
> *The petals of the clock*
> *Decay*
> *And years become minutes...*
> > *Chorus: Take me there, through the woods*
> > *Take me the way through the woods*
> > *Don't get lost*
> > *The sea awaits...*
> *Time will find you*
> *Will destroy you...*
> *Fragments of the world*
> *Surround you everywhere...*
> > *Bridge: The petals on your grave*
> > *By the ruined church*
> > *It could not last... Oh no, baby, it couldn't...*
> > *Chorus: Take me there, through the woods*
> > *Take me the way through the woods*
> > *Don't get lost*
> > *The sea awaits...*

Something Peculiar

from

John Langan

Acolytes of the Famished Giant

"…stabbed by a line of smiles…"

1980

NINE O'CLOCK and the broad Scottish sky still full of light. At home, in New York, Poughkeepsie, it would have been dark by now, the air hot, laden with humidity. If you tried to sit out on the back porch, mosquitoes would float around you with the lazy wobble of ashes drifting away from a campfire. You would hear their whine dopplering closer, to one ear or another, then feel a bite someplace completely different, your forearm or calf. There were no mosquitoes here in Greenock, though an alarming number of bees circulated among the bright flowers of the assorted plants crowding the strip of green grass Aunt Catriona and Uncle Rob called their back garden. It was another of the differences Alan (almost 12) noticed between the town where his parents had grown up and the city in which they lived with him, his younger brother, Francis (9), and his younger sister, Helena (2½).

For the first couple of days after their flight landed in Prestwick, he had kept a tally of the disparities between home and the place to which Mom and Dad had taken him several times before; though he remembered those visits in disjointed fragments: having to give Francis, still wearing diapers, his underpants because the car their father rented broke down somewhere and Dad had to flag down a passing driver to take him for help, leaving Mom in the car on the side of the road with (then just) the boys, the younger of whom she had run out of diapers for, leading her to instruct Alan to remove his shorts in order to provide Francis a substitute diaper. The embarrassment he had felt at (maybe) five haunted his memory, an obscure sense of shame exacerbated by the praise his mother heaped on him for his sacrifice, her strident, "*Good boy*, oh what a *good boy*," shining a light on what he was desperate to have over. He recalled as well crying on the plane as it descended to the runway, unable to equalize the pressure in his ears, his mother unwrapping a piece of gum which was supposed to help but did not. He thought he had stood in someone's garage, looking at a large wire cage in which they (a girl?) kept a pet skunk, but that couldn't have happened, could it? Skunks weren't indigenous to Scotland, were they? Perhaps it had been another animal: his memory did not show him the skunk, only the cage, dark inside.

But his father's parents he did not recall, nor the aunt, uncle, and cousins of that side of his family. He remembered his mother's mother, but that might have had as much to do with the photograph of her Mom kept on display in the living room, which showed a stout woman with short hair and a squinting expression, wearing a plain, almost shapeless dress, a large handbag hanging from her right hand. Somewhere in the middle recesses of his mind, there was a gallery of faces that felt as if they belonged to his parents' home, most of them Mom and Dad's age, their skin lined, their hair struggling to hold onto its original color. Although their names might be preceded by "uncle" or "aunt," this was in the way of an honorific and not an indication of blood relation. The situations in which he had met them last were separate from the images of their faces wearing smiles of varying degrees, from a bemused purse of the lips to a broad grin.

In any event, none of them were here in this late evening sun, seated on the folding wooden chairs reserved for the adults, especially his Granda, his father's father, not yet returned from his job at the shipyard. High-backed, Granda Brian's chair was composed of a mass of metal pipes and pieces welded together into a shape that reminded Alan of the priest's chair on the altar at church. Two heavy to move from its place at the far end of the garden, it was streaked with rust, canted slightly to the right. The chair didn't appear very comfortable, which was probably why there was a plump purple cushion on the grill that served as its seat. Max, Aunt Catriona and Uncle Rob's youngest son, between Alan and Francis in age, had told his cousins in breathless tones that Granda made the chair himself, which Alan supposed was an accomplishment worth noting, but did not find as remarkable as Max clearly did. The previous summer, Alan's dad had taken down the wooden porch outside their back door in a single long weekend, and replaced it with a stone patio the following weekend, feats that seemed to him as (if not more) impressive than making a chair.

On the other hand, Granda Brian had assembled his chair in the aftermath of his accident two years ago, when he had been struck by a bus while crossing the street on the way to the bookie's and suffered catastrophic injuries, coming within clear view of death. The accident had sent Dad out of the house and across the Atlantic for a long four weeks, urged to go by Mom, even though Helena was just six months old. Following his return, Dad refused to describe Granda's injuries to Alan, insisting they were too terrible for him (and Francis) to hear. But Alan learned of them anyway, due to the thinness of the wall separating his and Francis's room from their parents' and Dad's tendency to speak loudly when he was emotional. Thanks to architecture and volume, Alan discovered that his grandfather had suffered a broken forearm, shoulder, ribs, hip, and leg, all on the left side. More concerning, according to Dad, were the double injuries Granda's head had suffered, first from the bus and then from striking the road. His skull fractured and his brain swelled, to the extent holes had to be drilled in his head to relieve the pressure. Dad was right: Alan had not needed to learn all of that, and for months his dreams had been plagued by a shadowy figure with an enormous, misshapen head and a bent and twisted body, who chased him through a house with too many hallways while gurgling that there were *holes* in his head, they had made *holes* in his head.

From the same late-night eavesdropping – although was it really eavesdropping if you couldn't help hearing it? – Alan had followed Dad's reports of his father's remarkable recovery, relayed in a voice thick with feeling. This dovetailed with Max's account of Granda Brian spending the later months of his convalescence, once he was out of the hospital and able to walk with the assistance of a crutch, sifting through local junkyards in search of what appeared to his family to be random bits of metal, which he kept at the top of Aunt Catriona and Uncle Rob's garden, which was where, a few months later, he began to sort and then weld his findings into the chair now awaiting his presence. The result of his labors reminded Alan of something from a science fiction movie, one of those old low-budget productions you saw on the local channels on Saturday afternoons when there was nothing else playing. He could picture it as the throne the king of post-apocalyptic society ruled from; though he did not share this with Max or any of the rest of his Scottish relatives.

Without exception, those family members treated the chair respectfully, even reverently. When Helena attempted to climb up onto it, a collective panic passed through them; even Dad, deep in conversation with Nana Kate, raised his eyebrows. Of the adults, only Mom did not register shock at Helena's trespass; although she perceived the reaction of her in-laws and swooped in to lift her daughter from the forbidden chair and carry her giggling to her seat at the opposite end of the garden, where she sat with Helena on her lap.

As far as the differences between New York and Scotland went – a list Alan abandoned after a couple of days, when it grew unwieldy – this was the most profound, the deference Dad showed his father, who did not meet them at the airport but waited at the house he and Nana Kate lived in next door to Aunt Catriona and Uncle Rob. Unlike the figure who had haunted Alan's nightmares, his grandfather was a broad-shouldered man with a square face, snow white hair, and blocky black plastic glasses, the sole remaining evidence of his injuries the metal cane he employed to help himself walk to shake Dad's hand. Alan was shocked to see that Granda Brian had more hair than Dad, the top of whose head was essentially bald, surrounded by a crown of brown hair he kept neatly barbered. Granda's hair was full, not long but not short, either. Noticing the difference, Alan felt vaguely ashamed, as if he had somehow betrayed his father.

From that first meeting, Dad was jokey with his mother, calling her by her first name, which startled Alan, who could not imagine speaking to Mom in such tones, let alone, addressing her as Lila. Perhaps thinking the rules were different now that they were in another country, Francis tried using Mom's name, but a bark from Dad clarified that whatever else might have changed, this had not. With Granda, however, Dad was quiet, deferential to a degree Alan had not witnessed with anyone aside from the priests at church, and even with Father Fred and Father Gene, he maintained a humorous if respectful rapport. While he tolerated Dad's teasing of Nana Kate, there was no joking where Granda Brian was concerned, no quips, no clever comments – unless they came from Granda himself, who greeted Alan and Francis with a deep, almost growling, "Hello, *Yanks*," in whose blunt syllables his grandson felt a mockery whose source he did not understand. None of the rest of Dad's family seemed to share it, except for Timothy,

Aunt Catriona and Uncle Rob's third son, two years older than Alan, who with a pair of friends dressed in the ties and blazers of their school uniforms had met him, Francis, and Max the day after their arrival walking opposite directions on the way to the corner shop and burst into a loud, off-key performance of "Yankee Doodle," which had drawn sharp glances from the women and men on either side of the street and made Alan blush with embarrassment and confusion. Max shrugged off his older brother's behavior, explaining, "That's Tim. He's a bit of a wanker." The incident had left Alan with a vague resentment towards his cousin, who in the days since had greeted him with a sly smile whose ridicule was as clear as it was mysterious, unwarranted.

He was wearing it now, standing across the garden beside his older brother, Julian, a cup of IRN-BRU in his hands (the soda one of the differences Alan had stopped counting, a sweet orange drink with an added, almost metallic flavor he could believe came from the girders the brand's slogan said it was made with). Julian was holding a can of beer (lager), which Alan didn't think his cousin would be old enough to drink in the U.S., but in Scotland was no big deal. Despite a perpetual frown, Julian was cordial, even friendly, staying up talking with Alan and Francis the second night of their trip, long after Mom and Dad and Helena had staggered off to bed. He worked on the other side of the Clyde, the wide river on whose southern bank Greenock lay, at the American submarine base there. His responsibilities included maintenance of the nuclear missiles on board the subs, and while Julian said much of what his job entailed was top secret, he had disclosed that the bodies of the missiles were largely built of wood. Alan found this difficult to believe and wondered if his big cousin was teasing him and Francis, but Julian seemed sincere, so he did not argue with him. The next day, though, as casually as he could, he asked Dad what the nuclear missiles the submarines carried were made of.

Dad said he had no idea but supposed they were metal. Alan could have gone further, explained the reason for his question, but Julian had offered the information about the missiles in what felt like confidence, and he thought he should honor that.

In the days since, Julian hadn't been around much, too busy with his fiancée, Nora, a cheerful girl he would be marrying this time next year. He looked impatient to leave this family gathering, which Max had told Alan and Francis took place every ten days or so, replacing the Sunday dinners that had been the family custom for as long as Max could recall. Alan was familiar with the ritual of Sunday dinner (usually roast beef and roast potatoes with a green vegetable a generous pour of gravy helped him choke down). As Dad told it, the Sunday family meal was something he had been raised with, as had Granda Brian, whose father, Great-Granda Lawrence, had brought it with him when he came from Ireland to work the shipyards on the Clyde. After his accident, Granda Brian had changed the practice from weekly to a schedule he marked on his and Nana Kate's calendar, then instructed Aunt Catriona and Uncle Rob and their boys to copy and follow. Such was the force of Granda's personality that his daughter and son-in-law and grandsons obeyed his decree (or possibly, Alan thought, they were so relieved at his survival they decided to indulge him). According to Max, the new gatherings weren't much different from the old ones, some prayers before the food and then a lot of Granda holding forth on subjects ranging from the activity at the shipyard, to local politics/football (soccer), which as Max told it were pretty much one and the same, to religion, also the same as politics and football. Maybe Granda talked about religion more than he used to before his accident, but Max didn't pay very much attention to what he called their grandfather's sermons: he was more focused on pudding (dessert), after which, he was allowed to leave the table and watch TV. Everyone else was required to stay seated and listen to Granda, much to Tim's frustration, which Max reported with a chortle.

Usually, Max said, their dinners were held inside, no surprise given the changeable Scottish weather; usually, too, they were not this late in starting; nor was Granda this late in coming back from the shipyard. From his father, Alan knew that Granda Brian prided himself on not working one minute more than he was being paid to, a philosophy Dad endorsed, a reason he had never taken the promotion to management at IBM, despite the increase in salary it brought. That raise, Dad said, was a golden handcuff, keeping you chained to your office chair after everyone else had gone home. Better to make do with a little less in the bank and be free to drive out of the parking lot while the sun was still shining. Following Granda's return to his job, he had been shifted from whatever it was he did on the ships (Alan wasn't sure; it seemed to have something to do with installing the electronics on the bridge) to a position more accommodating of his post-accident condition (Alan wasn't sure what that was, either, except that it involved going to an office). His new responsibilities, however, had not affected the routine Granda had maintained for decades: so Max had said and Alan observed during the last week. At the end of each workday, Granda took the bus that climbed the hill to the stop down the street from his and Nana Kate's, from which he walked home. Since his return to work, he had been met off the bus by Aunt Catriona and Fred, her oldest son, who tended bar at a pub near the waterfront called The Terminal. Alan had met Fred a handful of times, always on his way out of Aunt Catriona and Uncle Rob's front door. His impression was of a bland, almost blank expression above a white dress shirt and metallic gray tie. Max said his oldest brother was okay, but not around much.

Here, though, was Fred now, stepping out of the house's back door and holding it open for Granda behind him. A collective murmur of relief passed through the garden.

Given the lateness of the hour, Alan was surprised to see his cousin, whose duties behind the bar began around six (he thought). It was another example of Granda's influence over the family. The open door allowed the smells of the dinner Aunt Catriona had prepared, steak pie and roast potatoes, to escape into the open air, provoking a grumble from Alan's stomach. Fred's right hand hovered near Granda as he crossed the threshold and proceeded onto the grass, lurching side to side as he went, leaning heavily on his metal cane. In Fred's left hand, there was a bundle wrapped in what looked like a piece of calfskin. Fred escorted Granda to his chair, which he dropped into with enough force to shift it to the left. Once he was seated, Fred bent over and offered Granda the bundle. Trembling from exertion, his square face flushed, Granda raised his right hand, palm-out, and shook his head. Breathing hard, he said, "No, no, Freddy. You do it. Like we discussed."

"Aye," Fred muttered. He straightened and peeled back the top layer of the calfskin. Something winked in the sunlight. Fred's features were set in an expression Alan could not read; it looked as if his cousin were struggling with some great, difficult emotion. From the bundle, Fred withdrew a tapered length of metal – a knife, Alan saw, the blade polished mirror-bright, the hilt wrapped in black electrical tape. His cousin walked to Uncle Rob and held out the knife to him handle-first. With a nod, Uncle Rob took the blade. Fred repeated the procedure around the garden, removing a gleaming knife from the calfskin and offering it in turn to Julian, Tim, and Max, each of whom nodded and accepted it. He continued to Dad, who nodded as if he understood what was going on and grasped the hilt. Then his cousin was standing in front of Alan, presenting a knife to him. A thrill ran up his spine. Seen this close, the knife was less utensil and more weapon, a dagger, a stiletto to be carried alongside a sword. He nodded and reached for it.

"Alan," his mother said. "No."

He looked at his father, who glanced up from the knife in his hand. "Lila," Dad said, "it's okay. Go ahead, Alan."

"No," Mom said, "it is not okay. That is a dangerous weapon, and he is eleven."

"Mom," Alan said. "I'm twelve next week."

"Don't you 'Mom' me," she said. "Put your hand down." Fred glanced at Granda.

"Let the boy have it, Lila," Granda said. "You'll be careful, Alan, won't you?"

"Yes, Granda," Alan said, "I will." Before Mom could issue any additional commands, he gripped the handle.

"Alan!" Mom said.

"It's fine," Dad said, "Lila, it's fine."

"It is not fine," Mom said, "it most certainly is not."

The knife was heavier than Alan anticipated, the weight of the blade tilting it down, pushing the hilt up against the base of his thumb. He tightened his hold on the black tape, which was warm, almost spongy. The edges of the blade were beveled, its point tapered. You could slash with it, but it looked more like a stabbing weapon. Up the center of the metal, a design had been scratched, what appeared from Alan's perspective to be an upside-down crescent, repeated for almost the entire length of the blade. If you were on the receiving end of it, you would think you were being stabbed by a line of smiles. A darker substance, red or maybe brown, stained several of the crescents. As the light shimmered up and down the blade, some trick of the late-day sun made it appear as if there was a further image incised underneath the reversed smiles, behind them, within the metal's mirrored depths. The brightness reflected prevented Alan seeing it directly, but the afterimages floating in his vision suggested a figure like a man, a thin man.

In the meantime, Fred had moved on to Francis, who nicked his cousin's palm in his haste to yank the knife out of it. Hissing, Fred jerked his hand back and pressed it to his mouth. Mom was out of her chair, done relying on her voice to halt what was happening. Helena balanced on her left hip, she strode to Francis and Alan and, right index finger pointing at Francis, said, "You! Put that down right now!"

"Lila," Dad said, "honey."

"Right! Now!" Mom said, her eyes burning like blue lasers.

"But Mom," Francis started. Whatever appeal was to follow (most likely, "Alan's got one") was truncated by Mom's, "No! You are a child," she proceeded, jabbing her finger to emphasize *child*, "and that," directing her finger at the knife, "is dangerous. It is a dangerous weapon. A *weapon*. It has no place in your hand. Now put it down."

"Yes, Mom," Francis said, setting the knife on the grass beside him.

"Honey," Dad said.

"As for you," Mom said, turning her attention and her finger to Alan, who felt his cheeks redden. Tim, he could see past his mother, had progressed from smirk to broad smile, holding his knife out proudly for everyone to see.

"Mom," he said, "I'm *twelve*," offering his (imminent) age and by extension his position relative to Francis and Helena as the best argument for being allowed to keep the knife. How often did his mom call him her big strong boy? Wasn't this the kind of thing he could be trusted with?

"Lila," Granda said. His voice, pleasant but firm, seemed to surprise Mom. Back home, in America, neither she nor Dad was used to being interrupted when they were speaking to (yelling at) their children. For an instant, Alan saw Mom unable to figure out how to respond to Granda. Then she gave her head a little shake and, lowering her hand, turned to Granda in his metal chair. "Yes," she said.

"You're right, Lila," Granda said. "These are dangerous. A foolish lad – a careless lad could give himself a nasty cut. Or he could cut someone else." Granda nodded at Fred. Francis flinched and looked down. "I must beg your pardon, Lila," Granda continued. "I should have asked you if your boys could be trusted with such grownup things. I assumed Big Alan," Granda waved his hand at him, "and Wee Francis," another wave to Francis, who lifted his head at the acknowledgment, "had enough common sense – had enough of their *mother's* common sense to be allowed to hold one of the gifts Fred and I made for them. I thought it would be a nice surprise for the lads. Honestly, your boys have been so well-behaved, never once did it occur to me they might not be trustworthy. They seem like such good lads."

"They are good," Mom said. Alan's heart lifted at his mother's words. Before she could add to them, Granda said, "Aye, they are. That's because you've raised them to be. So maybe you'd allow Big Alan to keep hold of his present, and Wee Francis to have his beside him?" Mom opened her mouth to answer but Granda went on, "That is assuming, of course, the boys promise to be careful with the blades. Will you promise me that, Alan and Francis? Will you promise to respect what you've been trusted with? Will you? Will you swear it?"

"Yes, Granda," Alan and Francis said at pretty much the same time.

"Aye, there you go, boys, there you go," Granda said, smiling a bigger smile than Alan had seen at any point since their arrival, displaying his blocky white teeth. "What do you say, Lila?"

Mom frowned. "I say those are sharp knives," she said, "and you, Francis, are to leave that one in the grass and not touch it. Do you understand? I don't want to hear any crying because you cut your finger."

"Yes, Mom," Francis said.

"Alan, there is to be no fooling around with that," Mom said. "It is not a toy. Do you understand?"

What Alan wanted to say was, "I'm not an idiot, Mom." But there was no world in which this was a good response to his mother's question, so he said, "Yes, Mom," and held onto the dagger.

"I'm serious," Mom said. "No joking about."

"Yes, Mom," Alan said, trying to keep the exasperation out of his reply. As if his effort hadn't been enough, Mom narrowed her eyes at him, and for a panicked second Alan was certain she was going to rescind her approval. He could hear Tim's snicker, if not outright laughter.

"Lila," Dad said, "he said yes."

The glare Mom turned on Dad was of sufficient intensity to produce a third-degree burn. Dad did not look away from it. A surge of love for his father swept through Alan. Mom returned her attention to him and said, "You be careful with that." Without waiting for his, "Yes, Mom," she resumed her seat.

"Thank you, Lila," Granda said.

Mom answered with a tight smile while she adjusted Helena on her lap. "Aye, well," she said.

"I wonder if I might tell you a wee story," Granda said. "My Kate's heard it before. So have Catriona and Rob and their lads. Heard it too often, they might say: am I right?"

Nana Kate smiled and said, "Oh no, Brian, not at all;" the rest laughed politely.

Granda winced and shifted in his seat.

"Are you okay, Dad?" Alan's dad said.

"Ach, it's just where they fixed me up," Granda said. "Sometimes I feel a twinge. Or worse. Especially if I've been exerting myself in any way. There's all metal inside me, boys," he said to Alan and Francis, "did you know that?"

"No," Alan (who couldn't remember if he'd overheard Dad telling Mom something like this) said.

"No, Granda," Francis said.

"It's true," Granda said. "Swear to… well, swear. When that bus hit me, it left me all in pieces. The doctors had to use metal plates and screws to put me back together again. You know there's a metal plate in my head?" He tapped the right side of his skull. "You could stick a magnet to it."

Alan wasn't sure if this was true; Nana's, "Brian," clarified it as a joke.

"Okay," Granda said, "maybe I'm having a bit of fun with you, boys. But the story I want you to hear is about when I was in the hospital and the doctors weren't sure I was going to make it. Oh yes," Granda said, nodding, "I was in a bad way. Do you know, my soul wasn't all the way in my body anymore? The bus knocked it loose, and it was just kind of hovering over the hospital bed. It felt like floating in a river, a river big as the Clyde. I could see myself – my body lying bruised and bandaged, tethered to all manner of machines. I fancied those machines were like anchors, keeping me from being carried out onto the water. I watched the doctors and nurses come and go around my bed. I saw your Nana sitting beside me, your aunt and uncle and cousins taking turns keeping her company. I saw your Dad, too, when he flew in. He's a good son, your Dad, dropping everything to fly three thousand miles for his father."

Out of the corner of his eye, Alan saw Dad's face light with pleasure.

"As I said to you, I could feel that great river stretching out, its current ready to take me away. Do you know, Alan and Francis, that's what we say here when someone dies: they're away?"

Alan and his brother shook their heads.

"Aye, away," Granda said, "like they've left for someplace else, taken a taxi to heaven or hell or the like, to purgatory. To God, who is our dwelling place. That's how the Bible puts it.

"But that isn't how it is." Grandpa twisted in his chair, grimacing. "God isn't waiting out there for us. Or the Devil. There are no angels, lads, and no devils. No heaven or hell."

"Brian?" Mom said. "Do you think—"

"No," Granda said, ignoring her, "what is there is something else. Something very, very old. Older than your Granda, older than my Granda, or his Granda. You know, when I used to work on the ships, way up high on the bridges, there were times I would look across to the

Trossachs – those are the hills you see across the Clyde – and I would think I saw a figure standing there. Like a man, but bigger, a giant, the size of one of the cranes, bigger. I only ever saw it for an instant, the time it takes you to blink your eyes. The first sight of it I had, I thought I was imagining things. Why wouldn't I? What else was I supposed to think? Then I saw it again. And a third time. I never saw it often enough or long enough to believe there was anything actually standing in the middle of the hills. When I did see it, but, the details were consistent. It was thin, the way a body is when the skin shrinks to the bones. It stood stooped forward. Its face – well, it didn't have much of a face to speak of, just a skull with the flesh drawn up against it. No eyes, and the lips pulled back from the teeth. Sometimes, it was wearing what looked like a crown of antlers. Given how big it was, the deer those antlers came from would have been monsters. The giant didn't do much of anything. Mostly, it stared across the river, sweeping its great head from side to side, slowly.

"No one else saw what I did. Whoever was working next to me, I would say, 'Hey, what's that over there, in the hills?' You can be sure, if anyone had seen the giant, he would have said something. I had myself checked out by the eye doctor, my regular doctor. Everything came back fine. I wondered if what I was seeing was the Devil, on account of the horns. It didn't seem like the Devil, but who was to say? I spoke to Fr. Manahan, down at St. Mary's, but he didn't take me seriously, said I needed to lay off the drink. There was no monster standing across the Clyde, keeping watch. Made me feel right stupid, so he did.

"I knew what I'd seen. My Aunt Margaret had the Sight, or so my mother said. She saw my grandmother after she died, standing at the foot of her bed. Other things, too, Mother wouldn't tell me about. Said there wasn't any need for me to hear. Maybe Aunt Margaret had seen the giant in the hills. Maybe I'd inherited a touch of the Sight, myself."

Alan saw his mom shoot a glance at his dad, who looked away.

"Now," Granda said, "I expect you're wondering why I never mentioned this to you, Lila."

"Oh, well," Mom said.

"After I told your husband," Granda said.

Mom's face became still. "You did."

"Aye, your man's known for some time," Granda said, "haven't you?" Dad did not answer. "Almost since I had my first vision of the giant. You were in America by then. I told him during one of your early visits. I also told him to keep it quiet, which it appears he did."

"Honey," Dad said, "I didn't think it was a big deal."

"What he means," Granda said, "is he didn't want you thinking your father-in-law was off his head."

"No," Dad said.

"It's fine," Granda said. "I wouldn't blame Lila if she thought I was away with the fairies. My Kate did. So did our Catriona and Rob and their lads, the older ones. No one said so, but I could tell by their reactions. It was all right. You couldn't blame them, really. With time, they came to tolerate my visions. It was another one of those things families share, little secrets they keep. And after my accident..."

The knife wavered in Alan's grip, sunlight sliding up and down the blade. He was doing his best to hold it steady, but it was heavier than he realized when he accepted it. Since Granda started speaking, its weight seemed to have increased, as if whatever he (still) saw within it, below those stained crescents, was gaining in mass. As far as he could tell, no such difficulties afflicted Tim, who gazed into his knife with the rapt expression of a saint in one of the paintings at church.

Granda licked his lips. "Right, Alan and Francis. What's all this about, eh? I was in the hospital, aye? Floating above my body. Feeling the pull of what comes after this life, which I fancied was like a river, like the Clyde as it is here, on its way to the sea. I could just about see it, carrying all the dead away. Well maybe that's not so bad, I thought to myself. I was in no hurry to leave your Nana, or any of the rest of my family, but I could see what a state my body was in, all my injuries, everything the doctors had done to me and were still planning to do. I had more metal in me than a scrapyard. Frankenstein's monster was good-looking by comparison. If I came through this, if my soul settled back inside myself, I was in for a long recovery, for more pain than I'd ever known. We fellows like to act as if we're all hard men – tough guys, you'd say – but this was a whole lot worse than a punch to the face. I don't mind telling you, I wasn't sure I could do it. I had the impression it wouldn't be very difficult to let go and let the current take hold of me.

"There was something else, though. A presence, you might call it, except this presence was an absence, a great emptiness looking over the river of souls. It was hungry – starving. Old, too, so old a word like ancient doesn't come close to it. Before people worshipped the God we have now, before they worshipped the old gods the Vikings and Romans and whatnot had, before whatever gods folk had in the time prior to that, before the land was sheeted in huge slabs of ice, and the oceans rose and fell and rose again, this appetite, this god was what human beings offered sacrifices to. Gods are always hungry, always asking something from you, an offering. We pretend it's for our own good, but it's really about keeping the god fed."

Mom said, "I don't think the boys should be listening to this."

"You're wrong, Lila darling," Granda said, "dead wrong. What they shouldn't be listening to is the rubbish they hear in church every Sunday. What I'm telling them is the truth, which comes from first-hand experience. I hung in that space just this side of death, like a cork on the tide, and I felt that emptiness waiting for its meal. Waiting for *me*. Aye, it knew me. I had seen it all those times, those instances. At some point, it had started to notice me. I had stirred its interest, no small matter for a being of such age. Now here I was, within reach of its appetite. There was an eagerness to it – a personal quality – that was terrifying.

"So what did your Granda do, right lads?"

Stealing looks at one another from the corners of their eyes, Alan and Francis nodded.

"I spoke to it, the giant. Prayed to this old god. It was hungry, I knew. If it would spare me, I said I would bring it food. I promised – I swore I would sacrifice to it."

"I'm sorry, Brian," Mom said, "but this is too much. Frankly, it's ridiculous. It sounds to me as if your accident left you with significant brain damage, and I cannot believe none of your family here has tried to get you the help you so obviously need, instead of feeding your delusions."

"Ah," Granda said, waving his right index finger at her. "That's a very astute objection, Lila. Do you know, you're not the first member of the family to raise it? Will I tell you how I overcame my Kate's concerns, not to mention those of our Catriona and Rob and their lot?"

"Aye, that would be nice," Mom said, though her expression suggested otherwise.

"I shared one of my dreams with them," Granda said. "All of them, at the same time, the same night. I let them see the giant. Let them feel its hunger."

"A dream?" Mom said.

"It was more in the way of a vision than a dream," Granda said, "strictly speaking. But it did the trick. Nicely."

"Do you mean to tell me," Mom said, addressing her in-laws, "that Brian told you he'd put a dream – sorry, a vision in your heads, and you believed him?"

"Lila," Aunt Catriona said, "you don't know what it was like. Dad's telling the truth. All of it."

"I cannot believe I am hearing this," Mom said, "not from adults. I cannot believe it."

Neither could Alan, who stared at Granda in his chair (throne) of metal pipes and pieces with a mix of awe and dread churning his stomach. Was Granda telling the truth? If he wasn't, then why did Aunt Catriona say he was? Was there a dream of the famished giant waiting for him and Francis when they closed their eyes later that night?

"You should," Granda said. "Ask your husband."

Mom turned to Dad. "What does that mean?"

"It means I shared my vision with him, too," Granda said.

"When was this?" Mom said.

"Three nights ago," Dad said. He hunched down in his chair. "When I woke up the next morning sick."

"You're sure you're not confusing the effects of too much Drambuie with portentous dreams?" Mom said.

"It was pretty real," Dad said. "It felt real."

"I tried to share my vision with you, too, Lila," Granda said. "It doesn't appear to have worked."

"Perhaps my brain's not as soft as the rest of your family's," Mom said.

Alan's eyes bulged, his eyebrows raised. This was not how Mom spoke to anyone, even Dad when they were arguing.

"Granda," Tim said, "are we gonna have to kill Aunt Lila?"

"Hey!" Almost before he knew it, Alan was on his feet, all fatigue gone from his arm, the knife held out before him, its point aimed at his cousin's smug, smiling face. "Don't you dare say that about my mom!"

"Yeah!" Francis shouted, standing next to him. "You watch your stupid mouth!"

"What the hell is this?" Mom said, now out of her chair, Helena returned to her hip. (Despite the gravity of the situation, a small thrill ran through Alan at hearing his mother use bad language.) "Boys," she said, "come here. We're leaving."

As Alan and Francis crossed the grass to her, the knife lowered but still clenched in Alan's hand, Granda said, "All right, everybody, okay, let's calm ourselves down. There's no need to threaten your Aunt, Tim. You know who your knives are for."

"Who?" Mom said. Alan had moved in front of her, Francis to her side. "What does that mean?" She looked at Dad, who was still seated. "Exactly what is your father talking about?"

"Don't you worry about that, Lila," Granda said. "There's a chap Fred has found for us, a regular down at his work. A real alky. No one'll miss him." He laughed. "I doubt anyone will notice he's gone."

"Oh my God," Mom said.

"What, Mom?" Alan said. "What is Granda saying?"

"You know about this?" Mom said to Dad. "You're a part of it?"

"No," Dad said, "honey, no." He had inched to the edge of his chair, but remained on it, the knife in his hand like an afterthought.

"'No,' what?" Mom said. "You're not a part of it, or you don't know about it?"

"Lila," Dad said, "you have to understand."

"I believe I do," Mom said. She took a step backwards, in the direction of the house's back door. Although he didn't seem happy about it, Dad stayed where he was.

"It won't be the first time," Granda said. "You should know that. Our god is ravenous. And I swore to feed it in exchange for my life. After I came back from the hospital, it took a wee while for me to regain my strength to the point I could fulfill my oath. By that time, I'd already won over Kate and the rest of them to my way, to the old way. We used a cord to begin with, because Rob read that was how folk used to do such things, strangulation. It was more work than I expected. You've no idea how much people struggle when they're fighting for their lives." Granda smiled. "Shouldn't have surprised me, I know."

Mom continued her slow movement toward the door, Alan and Francis accompanying her, maintaining their respective positions in front of and beside her.

"The knives were our Julian's idea," Granda said, tipping his head in Julian's direction. Julian smiled in response. "The minute he suggested it, I knew he was right. The giant is at home in the dark, in the dirt where the dead go, in the places underground where metal is hidden in the earth. I think that's why I feel it so acutely, because of all the plates and screws in me. It was the reason I built this chair, to put myself in communion with it. As I was sitting here, I was shown how to craft a knife that would house a tiny portion of the giant, allow it out into the world to taste the flesh and blood of men along the edges of its new teeth."

The four of them were at the back door to Aunt Catriona and Uncle Rob's when the handle of Alan's knife burned with sudden, agonizing heat through its tape wrapping. He cried out and dropped the weapon ringing onto the walkway in front of the door. He stooped to retrieve it, but Mom grabbed at him, saying, "No, leave it."

"Uh oh," Tim said, his face full of delight.

"I'm afraid our Tim's right, folks," Granda said. "Our god is an all-or-nothing sort. Either you're with us—"

Without taking her eyes off the group in the garden, all of whom had left their chairs, Aunt Catriona and Uncle Rob to help Granda up from his chair, their four sons pivoting to Mom, Alan, Francis, and Helena, knives held low and to the side, Dad finally standing but walking quickly in Granda's direction, his knife still in hand, Mom reached behind her and opened the back door, which whooshed in like an airlock. His palm and fingers throbbing, tears threatening to overwhelm his vision, Alan followed her into the house. The warm odors of Aunt Catriona's dinner enveloped them. As the door swung shut, he could see Tim, Julian, Fred, and Max starting after them. Mom clunked the heavy lock and steered the four of them through the kitchen, out into the living room. Someone thudded against the back door.

By the time they reached the front door, they were running.

For Fiona

Something Peculiar

from

Guy Adams

Hollow

"...miniscule wood slivers beneath the brain's skin..."

FRET JUST wished he could see what the old man was doing to the tree.

The autumn sun was as thin as hope, its light falling all but pointlessly on Bigman's Hollow, the small copse of ash trees at the centre of the park. Surrounded on all sides by dog-shit studded grass – a despaired of pomander ball. One step beyond that, an encircling road of post-war brick boxes, yellowed wood-cladding bolted onto shit-brown plaster, plate armour of old bone protecting fuck all. From the sky it looked like a target, begging for the bomb.

Twenty years ago, the local council, brown nosing for votes, had thrown a few quid into the building of a children's play area. A joyless collection of laminate particleboard, plastic and metal, nesting on wood chip, that brought children starved of alternatives from the surrounding streets. Fret, sat in the sun-brittle bucket of the playground slide, stared towards Bigman's Hollow, watching the old man sink even further on his knees – praying, it would seem, to the trunk of one of the trees. The *sound* though, the *scraping*, it itched Fret's skin. He wished the old man would finish his business and go home.

Fret lay back on the plastic slide, tilting the world downside up as he stared long into a dishwater sky. Either side of him, marker pen news bulletins – 'Gaz sux cox' 'Saras a slag' 'bum Jax hard' – turned juicy promise into the punchy, brutalist shape of Latin mottoes. He raised his feet upwards, stepping down onto the clouds, flipping the world on its axis so he could stroll home beneath a grass and tarmac sky.

The old man's noise intruded.

Fret sat back up, got to his feet and slowly walked towards the trees. He wouldn't get too close, if the old man turned trouble he'd be on his heels. He just had to know. Tiny mysteries were the worst, minuscule wood splinters beneath the brain's skin.

The old man was in front of the central tree, the one with the hollow heart that (probably?) gave the copse its name. A beige raincoat, stained with brown watermarks, made him look like he was wearing the plaster skin of a flood-damaged house. His thinning hair had tipped forward like a parrot's crest. His hands clasped the trunk of the tree, pressing and palpating at the bark like a kitten at teat. His mouth was clamped on the wood. Was he kissing it? Sucking it?

As Fret drew close, the old man looked round, showing off a mouth wide and wet and bloody as a shotgun wound. Teeth, worked free of their roots by gnawing on the bark, jutted at precarious angles, one more chew away from falling like corn kernels to the blood-stained earth.

"Ungug," the old man spluttered, releasing a gobbet of gob to slide down a stubbled chin.

Fret was in the wind, an arrow fired towards the safety of home as fast as his legs could carry him. Behind him, fading, but not fast enough, the sound of the old man resuming his gnawing.

Back in his bedroom, everywhere you looked there were totems to safety. So why didn't he feel safe? On the wall, Monkey D. Luffy, pausing his hunt for the One Piece treasure, offered a grin so toothsome you could play his face like a steel drum. An army of Funko Pops stared wide, drugged dead eyes into nothing. His clothes tussled and coiled on the floor, littered like murder victim outlines. An electric drum kit, dusty tarmac plates, waited for rhythm.

The problem was, he could see the trees from his bedroom window. He could see the tiny silhouette of the old man, filling beetroot gum flesh with dirty splinters until his mouth bristled like roadkill hedgehog. If he opened his window, cracked the double-glazed airlock, he might even hear the noise. In his head he still did. Always would.

"Fret?" His mum, downstairs, "You in?"

He moved to the door of his room, peering down the tumble-down lattice-work shadow of the stairs. "Yeah," he replied.

"I'm heading out." His mum, adrift in a cloud of knockoff Chanel, face painted for war, rustled organza bows at him, sequins catching the dull light of the shadeless, energy saving lightbulb that curdled their hallway. None of it ever reached her eyes. "Drinks with the girls. Your dad's around."

But where? That's what nobody could ever quite say.

Fret nodded at his mum's back as she fought her way past the highly-strung PVC front door before *ker-thunking* out into the failing light of suburban hinterland. Good luck to her out there.

He listened to the house for a moment, to the syrup-thick spatter of silence that dripped off every magnolia-painted wall forming puddles on the beige, synthetic fur floors. God but this hollow box hated him.

He stepped back into his room and tried to avoid looking out of the window. Darkness was getting ahead of itself, bullying its way over the streets. Fret was all for it, he couldn't help a glance towards Bigman's Hollow where the old man's silhouette quivered like a beetle pinned through its guts. Please hide it, he asked the night, *please*.

Knowing he wouldn't be able to help looking if he stayed in his room, he stepped back onto the landing. The silence still muffled everything, like snow robbing the world of its spark. His dad was in here somewhere.

He crept out onto the landing, tapping on the walls to make sure they stayed up. You couldn't bank on anything round here.

He touched the door of his parents' bedroom, rubber bump of thick white gloss on bitten fingernails. It wasn't closed so a little pressure fattened the wedge of darkness that ran alongside it. He tried to sniff the trapped heat inside, see if the darkness was lived in.

"Dad?" Did the shadows shuffle? Was there a restructuring of air as someone breathed in and out? "Are you in there?"

In the darkness, someone coughed, gagged in fact, and Fret was caught between an inbuilt fear of intruding and the sense that this might, in fact, be An Emergency.

"Dad?"

The gagging crescendoed into an expulsion of spittle, bile and something far more substantial. Substantial enough, in fact that it hit the carpet with a distinct thud.

"Are you OK, Dad?"

Sensing something on the move, Fret glanced down and saw what his father's YouTube videos told him was a Scolopendra gigantea (Amazonian giant centipede if you didn't mind angry comments arguing against misclassification). Mucus lubed, it painted a pink and white smear across the polypropylene carpet as it scuttled for the light. Fret couldn't bear the thought of it being loose so he stepped back and pulled the door shut. But that wouldn't do would it?

Panic gets us moving. He made his way along the landing and down the stairs. Around him, the house inhaled, making itself even bigger, puffing up to the rarified, gasping inside of a balloon filled with stale breath.

Through the living room, with its false fireplace fascia – Father Christmas had never accepted the challenge of forcing himself through the mortar, like beef through a meat grinder – well-worn leather sofa, keeled over in the corner of the room like an executed elephant, slowly softening with decomposition.

Adjoining, separated by a sliding door made of concertinaed vinyl, thick pterosaur wing skin covered in dust and bad dreams, was his father's study. Melamine-layered lattices of flatpack shelving held all of his father's books and magazines, accreted wisdom on insects of all sizes. A crane-necked mic stand, in-between podcasting duty, bowed respectfully. Fret, easily-led, might have bowed back, but he'd just stepped on a piece of broken glass so was distracted by the all-but-impossible job of not screaming. The scream would let the pain out, but the noise would be so loud, so sharp, so brutal, that everything in the whole wide world might hear him, and that wasn't the sort of thing Fret could bear. He gurgled and contorted, pulling the shard free from soft, ruined skin. He pressed on the wound, turning the sensory volume up high enough for it to short out and become tolerable. What would never be tolerable, though, was the state of his father's terraria, shattered, ruptured, ruined and emptied. Where were the inhabitants? (Well, he knew were one of them was, brought up whole, on the run from the gullet and crawling around upstairs. Surely the others couldn't have gone the same way? Couldn't be curling and churning and melting in their new gastric home?) When did this hunger kick in?

Fret backed out, his worry so dominant that he didn't even think about the little red kisses his foot was leaving on the carpet.

Upstairs, a loud thud, someone falling out of bed perhaps, struggling in a state of digestive anxiety, bellied with bugs.

Fret found he'd backed into the sofa and the huge flat eye of the front window behind him made him shiver. He felt it staring. He was quite sure that, were he to look, the glass would be filled with the faces of all his neighbours. Head after head, poured into every foot of available space, a rammed pickle jar of staring eyes, faces smooshed into pucker and wrinkle. Yes. That was what was behind him, for sure.

They wouldn't catch him that easily. He inched towards the door and out into the hallway. He needed to find safety. Everywhere had teeth. He grabbed his trainers, cheek-to-cheek on the welcome mat, slipped them on and then, head down, flat out, ran into the kitchen.

The rear windows were clear and he opened the backdoor and made a break for it before that might change. His bike was at the side of the house; hoisting it up he aimed for the gate at the back of the house and out, out, onto the passageway that ran along the rear of this whole brow-beaten row of houses. It was redbrick and cat piss, dandelions and dumped mattresses, and he jumped on his bike and tore through it like a zip closing a body bag.

He shouldn't have looked over the wall. Surprise shook him enough to metronome on the bike, sending him groundwards, face to grazed face with dog turd coral and a crack in the wall that vomited broadleaf plantain. He got to his feet, only too aware of the sound of running coming from the garden beyond the wall. It had been Mrs Kieślowski, dressed in her usual yoga-lycra, dayglo demon of stretch and creak. His momentary glimpse had shown her, fistful of turf, clodded sod, feasting her face. Starving saliva had turned her jowls muddy, slippery shite throat, eyes turned to heaven.

And now she was running towards him, maybe he was tastier than the loam loafs she had been making? She jumped onto the wall and her dirt-clagged hands slapped brick. Fret froze, straddling his bike but watching her crest the bricks, eyes on him.

"Empty," she said, dribbling grit. "That's the problem. Always."

Then she sniffed, looked down at the rough crumble of the brick wall and, with a low-gut moan, opened her mouth and clamped on. She quivered and rippled as she threw every ounce of strength into her jaw, but still couldn't take a solid bite. As Fret – freed – rode away he heard her body-slamming the bricks, not giving up on her hunger.

Out on the street, she wasn't alone in her determined dining.

At number twelve, the Morgenstern twins appeared to be throwing morality and genetics to the wind, but it didn't take more than a glimpse of the blood to realise they were chewing not kissing.

Mr Staples could be seen in his conservatory, working his way through his ever-loyal labrador, Simon. Good boy. Best boy. *Tasty* boy. Thank God the howling had stopped.

Ms Franco, ever the dandy, was framed by her bedroom window, rifling through her wardrobe, a throatful of cashmere and a belly full of tweed, bristling roughage.

Morton, never a man to have misplaced his Turtle Wax, had the common sense to tuck in tyre-first to his vintage Saab. They were hard to puncture but the incisor bounce built a pleasing momentum. In truth, his guts were sloshing with the petrol he'd siphoned spitless when first taking a kerbside seat, so there was no rush.

Finally, his mum, feeding herself jagged Perspex tuiles from the bus stop. She found herself at an impasse, the first, brutal isosceles having blocked the way down her throat. Its points tented skin front, back and left, her breathing a buzzing, blubbering hum. Still she tried to get more in, pushing and jabbing at the lid that was choking her.

God, but this world was full of holes that needed filling. How it ached.

Fret pedalled and tried not to think of the juiciness building up on his palate.

Later, truly empty, he burrowed into the body cavity of a hedge and cried himself dry.

Hollow. Yes.

He reached out into the thick, creamy air and hooked his fingernail on the darkness. He pulled, the shadow squeaking like rubber until he could get a grip on it. Then, slowly, hungrily, he began to swallow down the night, knowing there would never be enough of it to satisfy.

Something Peculiar

from

Web

"…things of such complexity and beauty…"

WHEN I was five I found a spider spinning a web in a corner of my bedroom. It had a small body and long, fragile legs. I grabbed it to show to my parents. *Look*, I wanted to say; *Look at this living thing that has chosen my room, that has chosen me*, but by the time I had got downstairs I'd crushed it to death in my small, sweaty fist. I was always anxious, after that, about my ability to keep things alive, an anxiety only worsened by a succession of prematurely deceased hamsters (who my mother said just wanted to die), then later, houseplants too numerous to count which would inevitably succumb to the pull of entropy. I vowed to stick to the inanimate.

I met Jon in my first week at university in Leeds, though soon he'd be Jonno, and later, Jonathan, as though he were trying to expand, to take up more space in the world. I appreciated this confidence, because it felt so different to my own way of existing. I liked the space he took up. It was winter when we started going out, and I liked the way he would enfold me into his coat so that I would vanish into his warmth. We would sit huddled together on a bench overlooking the fishpond on campus, the fish a vivid flash of colour amidst the grey bulk of the buildings and the spindly brown bareness of the trees.

I studied languages, he studied civil engineering. Through him I learnt new words: parabola, vector, torsion, shear. I learnt about density and load, about the secret mathematics behind the mundane things of our lives.

'It's civil engineers who protect us,' he said. 'Who keep us safe every day, even though most people probably never think about them.'

I would see echoes of him wherever I went; in the beams of bridges, the curve of a window frame, the angle of a roof. In lectures on the history of the Spanish novel I'd stare up at the ceiling of the lecture theatre and wonder at the forces needed to hold up all those floors of concrete above us. I wondered what would happen if someone somewhere had made a mistake.

We'd watch superhero films on a laptop in bed. 'That wouldn't work,' he'd say, watching Superman hold up a leaning building, watching Spiderman save a collapsing tower block with his web. 'The pressure's all wrong.'

'They're superheroes, the normal laws of physics don't apply.'

'For them, maybe, but they should still apply to the bloody great building that's collapsing on top of them.'

We talked a lot about what life was like for superheroes. Besides having to grapple with the unpredictable nature of physics, they had terrible responsibilities on their shoulders, which we felt were really very unfair. 'What if they've paid through the nose to get a nice hotel and some well-earned time by the pool and then there's an alien invasion or a super-villain tries to blow up New York again and by the time it's all over they've totally missed out on their holiday – would they get their money back? Can they ever enjoy themselves, knowing that disasters are happening at every moment?' These things troubled us; it wasn't the way the world was supposed to work.

'It's bad enough trying to hold down a job, what with all the demands on their time.'

There were many things that seemed unfair to us, including the eventual, inevitable need for everyone – even superheroes, presumably – to earn a living. But this was in the future. For now, we were blissfully unburdened by responsibility.

In my third year I went to Spain to study. Jonathan (he had grown out of Jonno by now) spent a fortune on plane tickets to come and visit me. We wandered together around palaces of mosaics and water gardens, marvelling at the human ability to create things of such complexity and beauty. We walked beneath orange trees just beginning to blossom. I pulled Jonathan out of the way of a spiderweb stretched over the path, a bulbous brown body suspended in the middle of it.

'Nearly got you,' I said. 'Thank god they don't grow so big in Leeds.' I gave a theatrical shudder, and Jonathan laughed and put his arm around me, and I felt happy and protected.

'It's more scared of you than you are of it,' he said.

I knew that. I knew it because I wasn't scared of spiders – not at all, and I felt guilty for pretending; guilty for making Jonathan feel like he was protecting me, when I was pretty sure he genuinely was scared of them. It was just that I wanted that feeling – that sense of someone looking out for me, of preventing disasters from happening. I would never have told this to anyone, of course. It wasn't what you were meant to feel.

We walked on but I glanced back. The web was enormous. 'A spider palace,' I said. As if it were saying, in the shadow of such grand human architecture, *I can do this, too*.

The truth was, my family had always had a thing for spiders. Gran had a spider story that was the stuff of legend, from when she and Granddad lived out in China, after the war.

'It were a monster, a bloody monster. Spun its web right across the balcony – nobody could go out there for months.'

I used to shudder in delighted horror and beg her to tell the story again and again.

'I wouldn't let him kill it, though. It's one of God's own creatures, I told him, and besides, I'd got used to it, in a funny kind of way. Even gave it a name. Attila.'

Attila. I'd roll the name around on my tongue, imagine an armoured spider, huge and implacable.

'Mind you, Attila would've taken some killing. Reckon he'd have fought back. I told Arthur – you go out there with a spade if you want, but I don't like your chances.'

She liked to tell this story whenever someone bragged about a close encounter. Attila one-upped them all. He fought off all pretenders with his sheer enormity, his chutzpah, hanging there over the balcony, his epic giving no fucks.

Gran used to say that she still thought she saw him, sometimes, decades and continents later – a silhouette on a white wall that would turn out to be a shadow or a moth; a scuttle of something across the floor if she opened a door too quickly. She said that she liked to imagine him living still. A constant in a changing world.

Jonathan and I stayed in Leeds after graduation, renting small, cheaply furnished rooms in crowded houses, their living rooms turned into bedrooms, their bathrooms blooming with mould.

The superheroes got us through.

'The Disinfector to the rescue!' Jonathan, in the bathroom door with rubber gloves, a face mask, and two bottles of Super Strength Eco Bathroom Cleaner.

'He might need to work on his name. And his superhero outfit.'

'But first he will work on the mould!'

Superheroes don't have glamorous lives, we agreed, but they made other people's lives better.

'And we love them for it,' I said, standing on tiptoes and kissing him on his forehead.

Jonathan got a job in a small engineering firm, but one with good prospects, he said.

'I just need to keep my head down and work hard and I'll get promoted in no time, that's what they're saying. And the work will get more interesting soon.'

I got a job doing translation for a digital start-up. There wasn't much actual translation involved – it was mostly just correcting the AI generated stuff, but it was a start. We saved up enough to start renting our own house. No more shared kitchens, no more cleaning up somebody else's mess in the bathroom. Our own life was beginning; this fragile, precious thing we were making together, building carefully so that it could hold us up and keep us safe forever.

My parents loved Jonathan, right from the beginning. 'It's nice that he's a practical person,' said my mum. 'Helpful to have around. It's so nice what you two have together.'

Because I wasn't a practical person, was what she was suggesting. I knew that. I knew that I was too careless. Too lacking in the things that a real person should have.

'Also, he makes you happy,' said my mum. 'That's all we want, for you to be happy.'

He did make me happy. Not in a swooning, intense way, perhaps. Not in the way that I saw in films. But in a safe, comforting way. In his attentiveness. In the small touch on my back to reassure me of his presence.

In May the wild garlic burst into life along Woodhouse Ridge. We sat on a bench amongst the white stars of the flowers and the faint smell of pot.

'We're not bad, you and me, right?' he said. 'Not too shabby.'

'Not too shabby,' I replied, my fingers entwined with his. A dog raced past us then came back and stared meaningfully at Jonathan, and then at the bag of crisps he had beside him.

'Don't even think about it,' said Jonathan, and the dog gave a last lick of its lips then wandered off.

'Now *that* is a useful superpower,' I said. 'The Snack Defender.'

'Fighting off slavering beasts with my bare hands, to save the last of the Cheese and Onion for mankind.'

'Mankind thanks you for all your sacrifices.'

Sometimes, lying beside him at night, I would watch him as light from the streetlamp outside our window fell across the bed, and it was easy to see someone else in his face. I would imagine all the other people he might be. All the other strangers I might have met. And I would be somebody different, too. The strangers had strong shoulders and full lips. I slept well in their arms. Together we dreamed different lives.

The first time we argued – really argued – it was over a spider.

I saw it running across the dining room floor. A house spider, one of the big ones with brown bodies and crunchy limbs. I'd been setting the table, but I stopped when I saw it, and hurried into the kitchen.

Just as I came out, holding a glass and a postcard, there was a bang on the floor. A foot stamping down. He was standing there with an odd look of triumph on his face. *Look what I did.* But his face changed when he saw my expression.

'I thought—'. He raised his foot and we both looked down. There was a dark mess on the carpet. 'You're scared of spiders,' he said. 'I was trying to help. It was massive.'

'I was going to take it outside.' I held up the glass and postcard. 'Like normal people do.'

'Well normally you shriek and run away from them.'

'Exactly, I don't *kill* them, and I've never asked you to bloody well kill one for me, have I? I always ask you to just take it outside!'

Words were exchanged. Somehow, we'd managed to get this far in our relationship with never raising our voices, but we did now, even though I knew – we both knew – how ridiculous it was to get so angry over so small a thing.

In the end, we ran out of anger. He did it for me, he said, again and again. He brought down his size eleven shoe and snuffed out a small, unimportant life. 'I'm sorry,' he said.

We stared at the dark, gluey stain on the carpet.

'Accusatory, that's what it is,' he said, eventually. 'Out, out damn spot.'

'You deserve it,' I said.

Later, we decided it was an origin story. 'Captain Arachnid,' I said. 'Defender of Spiders. Born out of remorse for his past misdeeds.'

'He wakes from webby nightmares vowing to atone for his crimes,' said Jonathan, 'though his sins weigh heavy upon him, and he's to be found sitting in his bare attic room in the early hours, cradling a glass of strong liquor and listening to mournful jazz on a record player.'

I gave him a shove. 'I hope the spider ghosts make you suffer.'

That was the start of it. So small a thing.

Captain Arachnid (the original spider man) lives an unassuming life. His colleagues in the office (Complaints Department, where he is patient and a great favourite with the customers, some of whom ring in a complaint just to speak to him) would never imagine that he would be the one out of all of them to have a secret alter-ego.

He knows what it feels to be six foot three and what it means to be small.

When he shrinks into his eight-legged form it gets him through walls and into houses, where he pulls the plug on vacuum cleaners, short circuits the lights, tugs out spiders trapped beneath paint. In human form he scoops up the victims of bathtubs and other disasters.

He worries that people will start questioning the dropped piles of clothing. The nakedness when he returns to human form also proves awkward.

The killing thing occurred when we'd just bought our first flat, one of those big stone terraces converted into oddly shaped apartments that are so popular in Leeds. The stain remained on the dining room carpet the whole time we lived there and when we sold the flat I watched prospective buyers, sure that their eyes would go straight to it, and when no-one noticed I was gripped by an urgent desire to point it out.

Our new house had polished floorboards and bay windows. From a distance, if you squinted, you might think it was an old house, but up close it was just pretending. It even had fake beams across the ceiling. I loved it.

We talked all the time. We didn't have another argument, not like the spider one, anyway. We pitied the couples who sat in restaurants, unspeaking.

'Maybe their dinner's just really good,' we mused.

'Maybe they're communicating telepathically.'

'They're probably pitying us for our unevolved means of conversation.'

We spun stories. Captain Arachnid evolved from his origins through a difficult period of coming to terms with childhood trauma, to several tragic love affairs, and a number of dramatic returns from the dead. He kept us company on long car journeys and late wine-drenched evenings. We thought we'd never run out of tales to tell.

Captain Arachnid falls in love with the Bluebottle Woman.

'I love the iridescence of your wings,' he says. 'I love the delicate tremors of your proboscis, oh how I long for the whisper of your slim legs on the threads of my web...'

The Bluebottle Woman has a weakness for men with clever tongues and a way with a needle and thread. They go on dates to reasonably priced restaurants, though Captain Arachnid can rarely stay for dessert.

'The responsibilities...' he says one night to the Bluebottle Woman, over a bottle of Malbec. 'All those fragile lives.'

The Bluebottle Woman holds her glass of wine in both hands. She can see herself reflected in the dark liquid, and her tears make her eyes look bigger.

Metamorphosis is both a punishment and a gift, Captain Arachnid tells her, solemnly, and she wonders what it would feel like to wrap herself in silk, to grow into something else in the darkness and emerge, clean and whole and new.

After a year or so in the new house we decided it was time to start a family. People had been asking, and after all, we had all that was required – the house, good jobs, two cost-efficient cars, biological imperative. And Jonathan loved children. He would teach them (there would be two of them, definitely, he said), about how to build things. 'We'll buy them those little wooden blocks. And then Lego, obviously, they'll love it. They'll be little engineers in no time.'

But each month when it became clear that no new life was growing inside me, I felt a quiet sense of relief.

I told him I was sorry, that we should keep trying, and he told me not to worry, that I never needed to worry. 'We have time,' he said. 'We have all the time in the world.'

I started to spend more time at work.

My mum taught me my spider-wrangling skills. She said that when she was little she'd been fascinated by spiders but scared at the same time. ('It's fine to be both', she said.) There had been a spider's nest tucked into the upper corner of the dining room window, and she would stand on a chair to get a better look at the tiny black bodies gathered together in their sac. It was that missing 'k', she said, that made it into something delicate and rare, and she watched the bodies start to grow, and she felt sick at the sight of it but every day she stood on the chair to check that the bodies in the nest were growing. It had been a cold April that year, and frost patterned the window. At night she dreamed of the sac exploding at her touch, and the tiny bodies pouring out, far more than the nest could possibly hold.

A cluster of spiders. She'd learnt the collective noun at school, and to her small ears that was the noise their legs made – a cross between a whisper and a click.

When she could resist it no more she heaved the chair to the window so that she could clamber up and poke the sac with a tentative finger, but no leggy bodies poured out, only a shower of desiccated crumbs.

After that she kept watch over the spider, but it just kept on spinning its web and catching flies. She didn't think it looked sad.

Villainy doesn't come easily to the Bluebottle Woman. She tries to look the part – sews herself dresses of midnight blue – but she finds slinkiness a hard look to pull off.

She's not even sure why she's acting like this; leading him on towards disaster. Plotting. Everyone knows that evil doesn't pay, that the long arc of the universe swings towards the good. It's not like she feels very strongly either way. It's just the path she's on.

'You need to get out more,' say her co-workers, 'join a walking club, take up a new hobby, let yourself be selfish for a while.'

She's selfish enough already, she thinks.

'Why don't you try something new?' he said. 'Take your mind off things.'

But my mind wasn't on things. It was clear and satisfied. I should have felt a lack, but I didn't. An absence un-mourned, unnoticed. I felt guilty that he mourned it so much.

I took up Italian lessons, though, because he was so keen that I find something new. I bought a beautiful new notebook, with a cover like a willow pattern dish that I loved, immoderately. After each class I wrote out all the new vocabulary, and at work I'd mouth the words *il cielo azzurro*; *il mare*; *la luna* and feel a wave of well-being sweep over me.

'Let's go to Italy at Christmas,' I said. 'Florence, Venice, wherever you want. I promise that I can order the best food and the best wines known to humanity. It'll do us good to get away for a bit.'

He put his arms around me and I imagined us there, in Piazza Signoria, the words from my notebook hanging frosted in the cold air, imagined us walking through long galleries of crucifixions and patient saints.

'But if we're getting the kitchen done...' he said, pulling away. 'And it's costing so much. And there might be more costs to come soon, maybe.' He said it with a little, hopeful smile that made my pictures of Florence vanish. 'Perhaps it would be better to wait until next year. See what happens.'

'Okay,' I said. 'Okay. As long as you're sure.'

'I'm sure,' he said. 'We're sure, right?'

Like all superheroes, Captain Arachnid is haunted by his failures. They crowd his sleep with their swelling bodies, with their whispery, disappointed legs.

'I'm sorry,' he tells them. 'I'm so, so sorry.' But they have no sympathy for his regret.

'I tried so hard,' he says. 'It was just never enough.'

'It never is,' says the Bluebottle Woman. She is holding a gun. 'You were doomed from the start. Why do you even keep trying?' Her feet are killing her in her new shoes and she can't help wondering why villains' lairs have so many mirrors. In them, she and Captain Arachnid are multiplied, fractured. They stretch into endless distances. 'Why don't you just give up now, Captain Arachnid?' she whispers.

He looks around, trying to find the original Bluebottle Woman. 'How?' he says, his voice cracking.

Things came to an end. It wasn't dramatic, it was just the accumulation of small differences. A thread snapped, there was nothing to hold us together. We couldn't find the same stories any more.

'Perhaps if we were a family,' he said. 'If it was about more than just…us.'

But also, perhaps not.

We divided things up in a fair and mature manner. 'It was amicable,' we told our friends, a word that neither of us had ever used before.

We said we'd go to dinner together sometimes, go to the cinema, though I didn't think we would.

'I'll miss our stories,' he said. He turned away before I could kiss him good-bye.

I missed our stories, too. They had been the pillars and beams that held us up. Without them, I felt unprotected, vulnerable to the elements. I stayed inside, ignoring messages from friends and family. I felt myself unravelling. I had never learned, I realised, how to live my own life. Too busy living a double life – one that never had just me in it.

'I don't know what to do next,' I whispered to my mum, down the phone, and felt like a failure.

She started to talk about new beginnings, and being young, but I had stopped listening, because a spider had appeared in front of me, spinning and spinning its way down from the ceiling to land at my feet.

'Sweetheart, are you still there?' My mum's voice was faint, at the other end of the phone. 'Have you left the house today, at least? Maybe you should come and stay with us for a while—'

The spider set off across the floor. It was a house spider – bigger than most people would want to hold, but still very small. I watched it run to the other side of the room and up the wall.

'Do you remember Attila?' I said, into the phone.

'Gran's spider? Of course I remember.' My mum's voice was fond. 'He grew in size every time she told that story. Don't want to think how big he'd be now, if she was still here to tell it.'

Superheroes are ideas, and thus they live cyclical lives. Their origin stories are innumerable, and swim in and out of focus like an old family video recording. They always get a chance to do it differently next time.

Captain Arachnid squats in the ruins of his web. There is only one thing left for him now. He feels his limbs transform from four to eight, his eyes multiply, coarse hair sprouts from his skin. The world fragments into light and dark and movement. He grows. He is the size of a house, he is still growing, he is looking down from a very great height and his knees, angled above him, take out a line of telegraph wires. His joints ache. The ground cracks beneath his weight.

The Bluebottle Woman weeps for him. After this come the cannons and the guns.

They try to capture him to study, but he is nobody's specimen. The only fitting end for monsters is in flames.

Wait.

This isn't Captain Arachnid's story anymore.

In the aftermath of apocalypse, the city is woven into a web. Silk stretches from the Corn Exchange to the Civic Hall, from the University tower to the radio mast on Emley Moor. The people of Leeds move slowly, as if they are under water. One woman starts to climb. She is afraid of falling but she climbs still. She finds the threads are sticky beneath her hands. She finds that the threads lead her backwards, back to a moment before the spider and the shoe, back to a girl with her eye to a spider's nest, to a woman raising a glass to the ghost of an eight-legged monster; to a balcony where a giant spider is holding court, his limbs spread wide as though he is trying to wrap a web around the sun.

Something Peculiar

from

Emma J Gibbon

Seven Encounters with Peculiar Hawkins

"…like a wisp of smoke or pollen…"

THE FIRST time I saw her, and she would argue differently, was at a house party of the girl I was seeing's friend's neighbour. I knew everyone there well enough to not feel too awkward, but not enough to actually enjoy myself. The girl I was seeing knew everyone. She moved from group to group air kissing them, and it vaguely annoyed me. It was one of the reasons I split up with her – the vague annoyance, I mean, not the air kissing. But back then we liked each other well enough, and I knew it was me being a miserable bugger as per usual. I watched her dance from one group to another, like a bee collecting nectar, while I stood in the corner nursing a Stella and smiling noncommittally to anyone who looked my way. I didn't like these people enough to have a conversation, so when I saw Jason making a beeline for me, I mouthed 'Going for a piss' over the music as I began to move to the other room.

Peculiar Hawkins sat on an easy chair in the living room, a semi-circle of women at feet. She was that kind of excessively thin, spindly woman with a flat chest that I was particularly attracted to but pretended I wasn't.

Her feet were bare, and I could see from across the room a dark smudge of a tattoo on her ankle. She kept reaching down and rubbing her feet, cold probably. That night she had on one of those shapeless sleeveless hippy dresses with some kind of ethnic belt cinching her non-existent waist. Her hair back then was a bright tomato red that I found revolting. Later, not that night, she told me it was aposematism, where toxic prey advertizes the fact to predators.

"Do you really see yourself as prey," I said.

"Perhaps," she said, "but I notice you had no problem with toxic."

"I didn't mean," I said.

"Yes, you did. You're not wrong though."

But that night the women sat around her feet, the kind of women who you see at the school run. They made her look like an exotic moth in comparison. I inched along the wall so I could hear what they were saying. The stink of patchouli almost bowled me over. I got close enough to see that she *was* cold, goose pimples on her upper arms. I wasn't gentlemanly enough to offer my coat. I'd look creepy anyway. I saw one of the women pass Peculiar her engagement ring. Peculiar put it between her palms and rubbed them together in circles. She closed her eyes and sucked her bottom lip, then took the gold band with a stone between her fingertips, feeling it before popping it in her mouth. The girl whose ring it was flinched. Peculiar opened one eye.

"It's part of the process," she said. I thought her lisp was caused by the ring in her mouth, but when she spat it back into her hand, the lisp was still there. She dried the ring on the hem of her dress and passed it back to the owner, who couldn't hide her disgust.

That soon changed to rapt attention when Peculiar started talking, that now familiar rusted voice, her laugh like a creaking gate. She opened her other eye and focused on the woman.

"You're not going to stay here," she said to the woman. "I see an ocean."

"Ooh," said the woman, "I could do with a holiday abroad."

"Shut up," snapped Peculiar.

The woman's mouth clamped shut.

"I see a cold sea. You will cross it and not come back. You will not be married."

"But me and Jace are engaged," whined the woman.

"You will not be married. Next!" Peculiar turned away from the woman, who had her head down, staring at the ring that was now back on her finger.

I don't think my eyes could have rolled back in my head far enough. I must have made a scoffing sound. I was always bad at hiding my true feelings. My mum used to say my face had subtitles.

Peculiar whipped around and glowered at me.

"Maybe you're next, Anthony."

"Oh no," I said, "Don't get me involved in this." I held up my palms and began to back away. Her arm shot out with surprising quickness, like a chameleon tongue catching a fly. Just as surprising was the strength with which she grasped my wrist, her clammy cold hand wrapping around the cheap knockoff watch my brother had got me for my birthday, the cheap bastard.

There was the sound of a glass breaking in the other room, followed by drunken cheers. I idly wondered where the girl I was seeing was, before my attention snapped back to Peculiar.

"It's psychometry, Anthony," she said. "Don't be a miserable bastard. I know things about you from holding one of your personal objects. Metal works best. Even cheap, gold-plated crap." She winked at me. I could feel embarrassment flushing my neck and chin. I tried to yank my arm back, but she held fast. "Keep still," she said and closed her eyes. Her lispy voice took on a funereal tone. I understood she was mocking me.

"Now, Ant, that's what your brother calls you, right? You hate it. It was ok when you were a kid, but now, it makes you feel small. Oof, he's got way more money than you. Why's he buying you a cheap watch, Ant? Ok, you're not in love. Don't worry, I won't tell the girl you came with. That's ok, she doesn't love you either. You will feel love, but it will be… complicated. You're not in for an easy ride, Ant, but you know that, don't you?"

I jerked my whole body back, finally breaking the connection. "Nonsense." I paused. "Who the fuck are you, anyway?"

"Peculiar," she held out that frigid hand for me to shake. "Peculiar Hawkins."

I reached out and shook her hand. She extended her index finger and stroked under my watchstrap. I shuddered in revulsion. Her nails were long and scratchy.

"We've met before," she said.

"Yeah, right," I said and backed away. As I turned, Jason and the woman who had her fortune told were arguing at the bottom of the stairs. I walked into the kitchen to get another drink.

Later, I finally went for that piss, ages after Jason had run after his fiancée, who had stormed off. I walked in to find Peculiar and the girl I came with hunched over the toilet doing lines of coke. I closed the door as quietly as I could, leaving them there and pissing into the rose bushes before I left.

A week later, that girl broke up with me.

It wasn't until that night that it hit me. How the fuck did Peculiar know my name?

— 2 —

The next time I saw her, I was on the train coming home after a disastrous job interview. I looked down at the stupid too-big suit I'd borrowed from my brother. I'd spilt coffee down it earlier, and I was trying to figure out how to pay for it to be cleaned with money I didn't have, which is why I needed the fucking job in the first place. I was trying my best not to be upset, but truth was I was gutted. I'd sailed through the first interview and the aptitude tests. I'd been convinced that it was in the bag. This interview had been with the 'team', ten to fifteen of them (I'd been too blinded by panic to know for sure) sat in a circle firing questions at me to see if I 'fit in'. A more perfect torture for me could not have been devised. Had I watched *X-Files*? How many times? What was my favorite episode? Did I play football? They had a five-a-side and practiced at lunch time. Would I join the team? Had I travelled after uni? Why not? Didn't everyone travel after uni? I felt myself mentally curling up into a ball. When they finally told me they didn't think I was the right fit, I couldn't wait to get out of the place.

Now on the train, I tried not to feel as if my skin had been peeled off. Everything was too much. The sunlight too bright, the noise of the train too loud, the sparsely populated carriage was still too full. A drunk in a tracksuit was starting to get rowdy at the back, arguing with no one. His ire rose in volume and intensity. I looked at the other passengers, hoping someone would intervene, tell the conductor, but no one would meet my eyes. Reaching a crescendo, he stood and threw an empty Special Brew can to the front, just as the automatic doors opened, and there was Peculiar Hawkins. She looked impossibly tall, and if anything even thinner. She stooped and picked up the can. She crushed it in her large hands (larger than last time, surely), and grinned at us all. Her hair was a sugary pink.

"It's all happening in here, innit," she said.

She threw the can back at the man with such velocity, I felt it whistle past my ear. The man grumbled but sat down. Peculiar bounced into the seat next to me.

"Hello Ant," she said. "Nice suit. I know a cheap dry cleaner, if you need it." There was no noticeable lisp.

Despite myself I smiled. "Nice hair," I said.

"How badly did the interview go?"

"Terribly… how the fuck… are you stalking me?"

She threw her head back and laughed her irritating laugh. I could see she had one of those old-school metal fillings on the left side of her lower jaw.

"I assure you, if I was stalking you, I'd be doing a much better job at it. We haven't seen each other in what, five years? I've barely thought about your existence since then, don't flatter yourself. You're wearing a suit that is so ill-fitting it is clearly not yours. It doesn't take Sherlock Holmes to figure out that you've been to a job interview. Plus, you've got a face like a smacked arse. It's not a wild leap to assume that you didn't get it."

"I suppose."

"Don't worry about it. It wasn't the job for you, you didn't want it anyway. Something'll come up very soon."

"You can't know that."

"Maybe I can? It's just a feeling."

She turned and faced the front of the train, conversation over. I looked out of the window, ostensibly to look at the fields and hedgerows whizzing by, but there was enough of a reflection on the glass, especially when we went through tunnels, to study her. When she thought I wasn't looking she looked older, more haggard. I felt something for her then, pity, compassion, something else? Whatever it was was a soft feeling, not one I was used to having. I continued to stare at her through the reflection. I must have been obvious, because she whipped her head around and glared at me, a penetrating, almost inhuman gaze that bounced off the glass. I vaguely remembered a poem we read in school, there were two women, and one looked at the other with serpent eyes and was a demon or vampire or something. I felt the name on the tip of my tongue. Just when I thought I'd got it, the drunk at the back seemed to rouse himself up again.

"Hey floss, floss, candyfloss," he slurred. "Oi, I'm talking to you. With the pink hair. Candy floss."

Peculiar sighed in a tired way but didn't look around. I sighed too, internally. Was I going to have to get involved in defending her honour, or shutting this fucker up, in my brother's suit? I didn't know if I was up to it, but knew I would have to make the attempt, or hate myself even more than I already did.

"Oi, floss, candyfloss. Look at me you stupid bitch. Don't pretend you're too good for me, you fucking c—"

"Look," I said, but Peculiar had already turned around, and was on her feet.

"What did you say?' she bellowed.

She stomped towards him. We went into a tunnel and as the lights flickered, it seemed she grew as she got nearer to him, not just grew, and I can't explain this properly, it must have been a trick of the strobing. It seemed her arms and legs got longer, like her elbow and knee bones extended. It made her look insect-like.

Then we were through the tunnel, and everything was light and normal again. Peculiar was standing over the man as he cowered in his seat. She was whacking him with a bag I hadn't even seen her carrying. She was screaming at him, each thwack punctuation.

"Don't you ever, ever talk to a woman like that again."

She spat at him. A stream of piss bloomed at the man's crotch and began to run down the floor of the carriage. She hit him again.

"You piece of shit."

She turned and walked back to her seat. She plopped down for the second time, turned and gave me the sweetest smile she would ever give me. She rummaged in her bag and produced a pen.

"Here, let me give you the name of that place that'll clean your suit."

She grabbed the ticket out of my hand and scribbled on it. Her nails were dirty and chewed down to the quick.

Then it was her stop, and she was gone again. I'd had the urge to get her number, but why? I wasn't even sure if I liked her. She gave me the creeps, truth be told.

My stop was four stops away. The drunk was asleep when I got off. At least I hoped he was asleep. I stood on the platform, watching the train trundle away. I threw away my ticket as I walked out of the station. Let my brother clean his own fucking suit.

Later that night, an old school acquaintance, Jez, texted me to offer me a job at his place. I said yes without even thinking about it.

— 3 —

For a long, long time, I saw her everywhere. At the train station across the rails, disappearing up a flight of stairs, down an escalator in town, at the end of the bar and then gone again, through a shop window as I waited for change. Her face always turned away, her hair a different colour. Each time, I chased after her, just missing her, and she disappeared like a wisp of smoke or pollen. I would think I heard her creaking laugh across a room, something unmistakably hers, but she was nowhere to be found, or I'd catch a whiff of that god awful patchouli and try to follow the scent like a bloodhound, but nothing.

I'd dream about her, hearing her call my name in my sleep, startling awake to nothing. Just my pathetic little bedroom in the pathetic little flat I rented with the money from my new job.

My brother didn't give a fuck about the suit.

— 4 —

Once my job ceased to be new and Jez moved to the branch down south, I was given his job and office. That beige box of a room made the futility of my work even more apparent. I spent a lot more time than I liked to admit just staring at my computer screen, or playing phone games, or looking at the ceiling tiles as I spun around slowly in my office chair. I wasn't the most dynamic employee, but I got the job done, so I was left to my own devices perhaps more than I should have been. One thing kept echoing in my head: *I've barely thought about your existence since then.* She hadn't thought of me at all, yet why did I think of her so much? I told myself that I didn't like her, that I was borderline repulsed by her, that I wasn't that attracted to her. I'd hallucinated that she was some kind of monster (due to stress probably). And yet, I protested too much, didn't I? I needed to forget about her. I had no way to contact her. No way of knowing if I would ever see her again. Did she know my last name? How come I didn't know where she lived? That couldn't be her real name, surely. Once again, I willed myself to stop thinking about her, but then I looked up at the cursor blinking on the Google page on my screen, and I leant forward and typed in her name.

There were no results. Nothing. How could someone have no trace on the internet? Not on social media, not on image search, not on local news. Nothing. Like she was a ghost… or a cryptid.

I resolved not to think about her. She was a lost cause. I didn't need any more of those in my life.

— 5 —

I followed Jez down south. He moved with his family to the suburbs, and I rented his flat. Smaller than the last, but more money. I commuted to the new office every day. Not so beige this time, a few pot plants and a window. I met a woman at a wine bar around the corner from the office. Her name was Nicole. She was a little older than me, accomplished. I was intimidated by her, truth be told, but I couldn't shake the feeling that she had chosen me, and I hadn't had much of a say in it. I felt hunted down, more prey than predator. We talked about moving in together, but even though her place was much nicer than mine, I dragged my heels. God knows why. I kept that small but expensive apartment, even though I was spending every night at hers.

One Sunday morning, as we were lying in bed in her pristine white sheets, she turned to me and said: "Do you think I'm too old?"

I reflexively said no without thinking about it.

"You have to say that," she said, but she was smiling. "Look at this." She put her fingertips under her eyes and began to move the skin around. "Look at how loose my skin is. Look at these wrinkles."

I smiled back at her. "You're fine," I said.

She rolled her eyes. "I am not. I'm haggard."

I was instantly transported to years before, on the train. Peculiar's face in the reflection on the train window. The way she had turned and given me that look. I knew now that I had been frightened by that look but had blocked it out. I shook my head to dispel the image.

"See, you're revolted."

I shook my head again to say no.

"Yes, you are. I'm going for that Botox appointment next week."

"What Botox appointment? You already booked it? Why are you asking me then?"

She pouted. "I just wanted to know what you thought, and now I know. It won't be too extreme. I'll just look 'well rested'."

"You know it's poison they inject into you, right?" I said. "Literal botulism."

"That's not literal. That's the food poisoning, not the toxin."

"Listen to yourself. A toxin. In your face."

"Forget it, Anthony. It's not your business." She turned over so her back was facing me. I don't know how I always managed to say the wrong thing.

All that week I had nightmares of choking. Something would get in my mouth and block my airway. I would start gagging. One night it was moths, so many moths, flying into my mouth. I couldn't spit them out, there were too many. As I opened my mouth to cough, more would fly in. Another night, it was strips of white fabric, much like my girlfriend's bed sheets. They were coiled in my mouth, and I pulled and pulled on them, the cotton wet with saliva, but they were never ending. Next it was hair, so much hair, multicolored strands clogging my throat like a drain. I didn't know what any of this meant. I considered getting an appointment with a doctor, but what would I say? I'm having bad dreams? I'm haunted by a woman I've only met twice? I was a mess from not sleeping well, but it seemed like my own fault. My own brain tormenting me.

I'd forgotten all about the appointment until Nicole came in grinning. I was getting a beer out of the fridge, and she made a flourishing motion under her chin, like a game show hostess. I looked at her closely and saw that she had some red injection marks on her face, a few small bumps, and a little puffy, but nothing as extreme as what I'd expected.

"You can't really see the benefit yet," she said. "It'll be a couple of days before it's noticeable." I nodded. I was acutely aware that if I was to say the wrong thing, it could really ruin the rest of our night. It was Friday, and I was looking forward to the weekend.

"Are you happy with it," I said, wincing because I didn't want her to take it the wrong way.

"I am," she said, "I think. I'll know for sure in a couple of days. It didn't hurt as much as I thought it would."

She took the beer off me. I let her and grabbed another.

"Oh," she said, "The woman who did my injections knew you."

I cracked open my beer. "What?" I said. But part of me knew, knew who she was going to say.

"Yeah, she had a really weird name. Began with a P. Not a real name, a word that's not usually a name. I was scrolling through my phone, and she noticed your picture. She definitely did know you. She mentioned you by name. Now, what did they call her?"

"Peculiar?" I said, trying to keep my face and voice as neutral as possible.

"That's it! Peculiar Hawkins. What a weird name. That can't be her real name, right? Or is she one of those people with bonkers parents? I was nearly called Buttercup. Like a cow."

"I don't know her that well," I said. "We just knew some of the same people back home."

"She didn't have your accent. She seemed to know you pretty well."

"I don't know what to tell you."

"She had the most vivid blue hair."

I changed the subject, and she didn't say anything else about it until later.

That night I lay in bed awake until it began to get light outside. I couldn't even begin to parse out how I was feeling. Excited, freaked out, scared? All of the above and then some. I told myself I would find out where the clinic was just so I could avoid it, obviously. Only then did I begin to nod off.

— 6 —

It was a couple of weeks later when my girlfriend dragged me to a dinner party at a fancy townhouse in the suburbs. Someone she knew from uni. We'd been there before for… something. I don't remember what exactly. They were always having little shindigs at their house. I didn't fit in with these people. It didn't matter about how much money

I made, or even what status I had at work. I had the stink of the working class about me, and a northerner to boot. To them I was a caricature, a novelty. They poked fun at the way I talked, implied I was stupid, and then got all wide-eyed and put out when I had the temerity to be offended. I avoided them as much as I could, but I was still a tiny bit in the doghouse over the whole Botox thing, and Nicole kept asking me about Peculiar. Something about my responses wasn't satisfactory to her. She wouldn't leave it alone. She kept needling me about it, like a wasp stinging me over and over.

So, I had reluctantly agreed to go to the dinner party, to show willing and all that. We stood outside the door, and she rang the doorbell. As we were buzzed in, she turned to me, and said:

"They're having a séance. Did I tell you that?"

"No, you didn't," I said through gritted teeth. She knew I would never have agreed to it if she'd said.

We walked down the narrow passageway and were ushered into the dining room by the hosts. It looked different since the last time we were there. They'd really committed to the theme. The big light was shut off, and way too many lamps circled the room with fringed silk scarves over them. It had to be a fire hazard. It felt claustrophobic, and I inwardly cursed Nicole for her lie of omission. We sat at the long table and tried to make small talk.

The food was good, I won't lie. Fuck knows what most of it was. A series of small plates put in front of me, the atmospheric lighting making it too dark to see well. My wine glass filled over and over again. I didn't even drink wine, but I wasn't going to ask for a lager and risk all of their stupid jokes. Besides, after three glasses it didn't really matter. We waited for all the smokers to come back in after dinner before the show started. I tried to get up and leave with them, but one look from Nicole made me sit right back down again. God, I hated all this stuff.

The entertainment was led in by the hostess, Cici. The medium was swathed in fringed shawls, one wrapped over her head like a hood. She was tall and skinny and looked like one of the dumb lamps scattered around the room. When she sat at the head of the table, I noticed that she was wearing gaudy dress rings on every finger. There was something familiar about those hands, and I knew before I knew, if you see what I mean. She uncovered her head and looked around at the assembled room. It was Peculiar, because of course it was. Her hair looked dirty green in the dim lighting.

She made no sign that she recognized me, but my girlfriend leaned over to me and said,

"Is that?"

"Shhhhh," said Peculiar in a voice that was a lot lower than the one I'd heard before. Nicole sat back and gave me another look.

"I can't believe you brought me here," I hissed.

Peculiar focused her eyes on me for a second, and I was again taken back to the train. What or who the fuck was this woman and why did she keep turning up? Dark lip gloss made her mouth look black.

"Everyone hold hands," she said in that strange, low voice. Everyone obeyed. "Feel the energy flowing through our bodies, making a circuit, creating the atmosphere conducive to the spirits."

Some bloke at the other end of the table guffawed. The woman next to him slapped his arm with the back of her hand. "Shut up, Ger," she said. The palms of my hands started to prickle and itch. Suggestion and the heat of the room, I reckoned. Peculiar closed her eyes and began to sway back and forth, then she reared her head up like a cobra, and opened her eyes, only the whites showing. Another voice came out of her. She had a Welsh accent.

"Gerald," she said, "Are you misbehaving? Why can't you ever take anything seriously?"

The man who had laughed went drip white. "Grandma?"

"It is. I can't stay long, love. Say hello to your grandad for me."

Gerald was stuttering. "I will, Gran. I will."

Peculiar closed her eyes, and her head collapsed down, her chin on her chest.

Another sound emanated from her, a very, very low growl. My girlfriend and I looked at each other in alarm. What the fuck was going on? There was a nervous titter around the table. Peculiar's head snapped up, her eyes wide and bright.

"Cynthia," she barked in a strong male voice. How was she doing this?

Cici answered. "Dad…"

"So, you married him, eh? No use telling you you've made a mistake then."

If her husband could have disappeared through the floor, he would have. I found myself enjoying one of their stupid parties for the first time ever.

"Dad, come on. I've got guests."

"And I'm sure some of them told you not to marry him, too." Cici flushed red. It seemed impossible we could see that under the lights. "Never took my advice. Never. Just like your mother."

"Keep Mum out of this," said Cici.

On and on it went. Peculiar had a different posture, a different voice, a different face for nearly every guest. There wasn't much that was positive. It seemed every spirit had grievance with the living. Old wounds were opened, dirty laundry aired. Poor Cici had broken the circle, her head in her hands. Her neighbours closed it again by clasping their hands over the table. Peculiar kept going.

"Nicole," she said, in a lisping voice I recognized as her own.

My girlfriend stiffened.

"He doesn't love you," she said. My girlfriend got up and ran out of the room. I was about to follow her, but the woman who had been next to her grabbed my hand and dragged me back down to the table.

"Ant," Peculiar said, still in her normal voice. "Anthony."

Oh, Christ, I thought, my brain running through lists of the dead who I might have pissed off. My brother had dropped dead of a heart attack the year before. I had grieved more than I ever expected to. Peculiar started coughing, choking, a horrible wet phlegmy noise.

"Is she ok?" said the woman next to me. I shrugged. "Isn't that your name?" she said. I nodded.

Peculiar groaned and retched. She reached into her mouth and started to pull a spit-soaked strip of white fabric out of her mouth, like a bandage, like the one from my dream. She pulled and pulled, plucking it with her thumb and index finger, an impossible amount to be in her mouth. How did she get it in there? She was talking moments before. She couldn't have been hiding it in her mouth, and she hadn't moved or taken her face out of sight of the guests. Was she regurgitating it? Bile filled my own mouth. It burned as I swallowed it down. Then she let go of it, but instead of dropping on the table, it hung in the air seemingly of its own volition. It snaked upwards and began to transform, changing substance like it was melting and switching color from white to a pale luminous green. It began to move and spread, tendrils reaching out towards the ceiling. It reminded me of an old lava lamp of my cousin's that he had when we were teenagers. It was one of the original '70s ones, and the paraffin wax had started to degrade and deform, looking almost fetal.

The woman next to me pulled me closer and said in my ear. "Is that fucking ectoplasm?"

"No clue," I said. I couldn't take my eyes off the thing. It began to make shapes. A huge bird flying across the room, a trumpet, a gargoyle, a screaming face. The same woman next to me fainted, her head banging on the table, her hand limp in mine. Still the stuff shifted: a cat, a voluptuous figurehead, a roaring bear, teacups tumbling in thin air, and then, impossibly, a huge praying mantis, a monster version of one I'd seen in a pet shop long ago. It moved towards me. I pressed my back against the chair, straining my neck to get away from it. It brought its massive head closer to mine and tilted it from side to side as if studying me. Its eyes looked straight into mine.

I don't think I've ever experienced terror like that before or since. It felt like the kind of terror that only people in wars or terrible accidents feel, a kind of existential terror, but what would I know? I could have been there for seconds. I could have been there for years. Any sense of time just left me. I was paralyzed, absolutely paralyzed with fear.

Then time sped up, and Cici was on her feet, and moving towards the light switch. The room was flooded with light, and the praying mantis dissipated into tiny particles and disappeared.

"Get the fuck out of my house," Cici screamed at Peculiar. Peculiar got up and left, and I ran after her, leaving the woman next to me still out cold.

I found Peculiar in an alley a couple of doors down. She was puking her guts out, gouts of stringy green vomit.

"What the fuck was that?" I said. She didn't respond. "Peculiar, what the fuck was that thing? Was it real? How did you... how did you manage that. It was a trick, right!? It can't have been real."

She raised her head to me, still retching, but nothing more coming out. She wiped her mouth with the back of her hand. "Take me home," she said.

"I don't know where you live."

"No, your home, idiot."

I did what she told me. I took her back to my barely lived-in flat, thick greasy dust covering everything. She got in the shower to clean up, and when she was done, she slipped into bed with me. When I made love to her, she seemed to be so fragile, all bones, and I was afraid I would crack one of her ribs or something, but then it turned into something else. I felt taken over, overwhelmed, but not in a bad way, like the opposite of the terror I'd felt earlier. I'd never felt that way before or since.

Afterwards, we lay in each other's arms, and she began talking, talking, talking. About hair dye and aposematism, about praying mantises and ectoplasm, fortune telling, Botox injections, and getting coffee stains out of borrowed suits, about where she'd been and what she'd seen, on and on, an accounting of all the times we'd seen each other, including the one from before, which I knew wasn't real, but didn't contradict her. I didn't mind. I listened to her husky voice, no speech impediment detectable, until morning light began to stream through the windows. When she had finally finished, her voice hoarse, I asked her what her real name was.

"Alison," she said. "Alison North."

"Your surname isn't even Hawkins?"

"Nope. Don't ever call me by my real name. I'll bite your head off."

I had no doubt that she would.

When I woke up later that morning, she was gone.

I never went back to Nicole's.

— 7 —

The last time I saw Peculiar was during lockdown at the beginning of the pandemic. I'd changed jobs, finally, moved to Manchester. I got a place not too far from the city centre. It was overpriced for what it was, but it had a tiny balcony, which I was fond of. It was early in the morning. I was about to log in to start work when I heard someone shouting my name. I went out onto the balcony, and there she was, looking at me. Her hair was pitch black, and it didn't suit her. She was barefoot, carrying her high-heeled shoes in her hand.

"I just wanted to say hello."

"Where have you been? How did you find me?"

"Around. I always know where you are."

"I've not seen you in years." It was the truth. I'd tried to forget all about it all, but it haunted me. She still haunted me.

"Can I come up?" She said.

I wanted her to. God, I wanted her to, but we were supposed to stay apart, right? Not spread the virus.

"You know you can't, Peculiar."

She nodded like she understood.

"I suppose," she said, and just as I was about to relent, press the buzzer to let her up, Covid be damned, she blew me a kiss, let out a peal of that ridiculous laughter, and ran away down the road in her bare feet on that sunny morning.

I haven't seen her since. That was what, five years ago, twenty years since I first saw her? You know how the pandemic feels, simultaneously two minutes and a hundred years ago. I'm used to time bending, though. My dealings with Peculiar have taught me that. Sometimes I fantasize about calling her name out, her real name. Let her come and rip my head off and put me out of my misery. For now, I wait, and I try to get on with my life and fail, forever looking over my shoulder.

Something Peculiar

from

Danie Ware

The Recollection

"...faded pieces of things lost..."

I LOVE these shops.

They're full to the brim, tattered rummage-fests of other people's lives, their loves, their memories. Some might call this stuff 'junk', but I adore it, and find it fascinating. I could walk through the twists and turns and hallways of these places for days, losing myself in the treasures I discover. Who really did sleep in a bed that crazy? Who's house was emptied of that many china cats? Who wore those clothes, hung those pictures on their walls? And why did that person own a *porthole?*

Every item tells a story, and I like to imagine what they'd be.

The store I'm in is huge, sprawling on endless levels. For every stairway, every nook and cranny, there's another arch or hall, and another, and another, going further and further back. I follow them like a person in a dream, losing sight of the windows and the light, and of anything resembling a till point. I see old posters, some for sale, others just faded pieces of things lost. There are scribbled notices telling me that there's more upstairs, or giving me the number for the house clearers. Ornaments stand on every surface, their porcelain eyes following me as I pass. Brassware glints – what even *is* that? – and locked glass cases are laden with old action figures, things I haven't seen since my childhood.

I stop, looking at the closest. I wanted stuff like this, when I was younger, but my family didn't approve. I was supposed to be a proper girly girl, into dolls and dresses, and dreaming of my one-day marriage, but I liked *Star Wars* and *Doctor Who*. I read science fiction books, everything I could get my hands on, and I watched all the classic movies: *Jason and the Argonauts*, *Fantastic Voyage*, *Journey to the Centre of the Earth*. Such films were rare, in the Seventies and seeing one was a treat.

I meander to another case, this one covered in dust. Within it, on the top shelf with a little tie-tag on his sandalled foot, is a miniature Talos, looking like he'll turn his head at any moment. Enchanted, I stand there like a chilled child at a frosted window, yearning for the warmth within. Then I catch myself at it, and laugh. I can't see what the tag says. Wondering how much he costs, I look round for someone with a key.

There's no-one there, not even other browsers. The place is utterly silent. I can't hear feet, or conversation. With a faint prickle of chill, I turn fully, scanning the walkways and corridors, but they're all empty. Wonder what the time is, I think the shop might be closing.

Faintly uneasy, I go to retrace my steps. I need to find the till, and speak to someone.

I turn three corners and – of course – get lost.

The inevitability of it makes me groan. I'd come up two flights of steps, I think, one wooden, and the other tiled stone. I'd turned left, then left again. I'd walked through an archway that still had a huge metal gate, almost garden-like, perhaps the remnant of something that had once been outside. In here, it's not only the stock that tells stories.

But never mind that now.

I keep walking, searching for something familiar. Had I come this way, or this way? I find another passageway, long and narrow and lined with clothes rails. It smells faintly musty, like the clothes have been here a long time. I see a long mirror, its surface blotched with black, and as I glance at it, a flicker of movement catches my eye.

I stop, my breath held, my chill rising.

What the hell was that?

I look round, but there's no-one there. Frozen to the spot, heart hammering, I count five, then ten, then look back at the mirror. It reflects only the passage, and, when I step forwards, I see myself. I'm wearing my padded anorak and flared jeans, both of which have seen better days.

Summoning my courage, I call, 'Hello?'

The lines of hanging clothing swallow the word. The air is cold, and the mirror stands there, dark and stained. Between its marks, I look out at myself, my face pale, my long hair haphazardly tied back and coming loose round my ears. There's not a shadow, not a sound.

There's nothing there, I tell my reflection, firmly. *You imagined it. Now, let's get out of here, before someone locks the door.*

Forcing myself to walk, I leave the mirror and the clothing behind me. My shoulders creep, like there's something still lurking, still watching. Something following me. Heading back towards the metal gate, I'm half-expecting the hallways to start moving, or something, swapping round like some mythical labyrinth, but no, everything's exactly as it was, china cats and all.

With a little concentration, I get back as far as Talos. Tiny, he stands there like a marker.

As I look at him, something moves in the glass.

This time, my heart hits my chest and I spin, half-crouching. I have nothing on me, only my purse in my pocket and my single door-key, but I curl my hands into fists. What I think I'm going to do with them, I've no idea, but the gesture makes me feel slightly better.

This place must be *haunted*, or something.

The chill is crawling up my spine, now, chill fingers on my skin. I stay exactly where I am, scanning the tessellated tangles of shelves and old furniture. There are hats, hanging from every conceivable edge and corner, scarves draped over everything. There's the top half of a male mannequin, naked and headless, and a box of very old LEGO, with a sticker that says '£40'. Its bright colours are oddly grounding.

Looking at it, I shake off the phantoms. *Just go all the way straight,* I tell myself sternly. *Sooner or later, you'll find a wall.* Thinking about breadcrumbs, I choose right and go and look for the stairs.

More corridors, and then more. A ladder into some kind of attic. A bookstall, the paperbacks all yellowed. A winding stone path, and an old wooden bench bearing a greened brass plaque. They seem oddly out of place. Soon, I lose all sense of time or direction. I have a wristwatch, but it doesn't work. It has Princess Leia on it, and I wear it because it was one of the very few things my family ever bought me that I liked. I've still not seen or heard anyone else, and I think the shop must be closed now. I want to call again, but the sound gets stuck in my teeth.

Hello? Hello? Is there anyone there?

Once more, I stop, turning round, and round again. I'm starting to get genuinely scared.

And once more, I catch movement from the corner of my eye.

This time, I turn to face it, trying to see what it is. I find myself looking a photograph, a black and white shot of someone's family. There's a severe-looking elderly lady, seated at its centre. By the clothing, it looks like it was taken in the 1920s.

The family are not moving. They glare from the image, but their monochrome smiles are fixed forever. No, what's moving is something at the photograph's edge, a ghost, reflected in the glass. It's a figure, slight in build and clad in black, its face covered by a hood. Even as I see it, it moves to the edge of the frame, and is gone.

The chill spreads out across my shoulders, and I shudder.

There is *something in here,* I think.

Or rather, something in there.

Old movies assail me: *Cry of the Banshee, The Dunwich Horror.* The Lovecraft books I've read, and my ritual 'rite of passage' perusals of *Carrie* and *The Rats.* I'm running out of ways to rationalise this. There's something *in* that bloody reflection.

And I think it's following me.

At the thought, my nerve breaks and I run. I don't care where I'm going, not now. I just want to get away from whatever that was.

But somehow, I can't outrun it. It keeps pace, fleeting flashes in every glass surface I pass. I think it's reaching for me, clawed hands like pure darkness. It's not real, it can't possibly be real, but I keep running, on and on, until I'm hot and short of breath and there's a stitch in my side. When I stop, dragging air into my lungs and digging my fingers into my flesh, I see it again, this time in a round, floral-painted mirror hung wonky on the wall.

The same black-clad figure, a hood over its face.

This time, it pauses. The head turns slowly towards me, just like the Talos figure didn't. I can't see its eyes, its expression, but it seems to stare out at me, its gaze burning.

No way. You can't be in there!

Ignoring the stitch, I lurch back into motion. I've no idea where I am, haven't seen any of this before. I pass an old sideboard and a pile of woodwind instruments, flutes and clarinets, all in cases with faded velvet linings. There's sheet music, too, as yellow as the books had been.

It's starting to occur to me: none of this stuff has been touched in years.

Where *am* I?

No, I tell myself. *Stop being ridiculous. This is still a shop, and there's a way out. There has to be.*

I pick up speed, running once more, but trying to keep rational. I still haven't found a wall. More encouragingly, though, I also haven't doubled back on myself, or passed the same thing twice. Which means I must be making progress, right?

Fears jump at me, and I struggle to keep them back. Every time I pass a glass surface, the figure's there, like it's stalking me, or trying to tell me something. When I stop a second time, my ribs heaving, I find myself facing a television, a great big, cathode ray thing, in a monstrous wooden cabinet.

The cabinet's doors are open. And the figure's there, it's *there* in the screen. The television's off and there's nothing else, only the grey-black backdrop and the figure at its centre. It's seen me and it's moving, coming towards me and reaching out its hands. It's trying to tell me something, I think. I stand there, transfixed, but I still can't see its face and it just gets larger and larger. As it fills the screen completely, it stops, its hands pressed flat against the inside of the glass, the pads on its bare fingers paling at the contact.

It looks like it's actually *in* there, trapped in some – what? – reflection-world?

That's crazy!

My mind reels. Impossibilities grab at me, making me stagger. All those old fantasy books are coming back to haunt me, now – Shannara, Elric, Thomas bloody Covenant – so many stories. On some level, I find that I almost want to believe what I'm seeing. Somehow, I want to know that there's more than just 'normality'. That there are layers, more worlds behind or above our own.

But no, that's crazy.

The figure hasn't moved, its hands pressed to the glass. We're staring at each other like a pair of separated lovers, enthralled. As I watch, it takes one hand away and starts to reach for the hood.

A creaking-metal noise makes me start, and my heart nearly bursts from my chest. My pulse roars into full volume and I'm running almost without volition, propelled by pure terror. For a moment, I'm not even sure if I'm running towards the noise or away, and then I understand that it doesn't matter. What I'm running from is that reflection, not only out of fear, but also out of some strange, newborn sense of responsibility.

Like there *are* other worlds. Like that person is somehow stuck and I have to rescue them, but I have no idea why, or how. Where to begin. I think I'm scared of failing, falling short of the fantasy heroes of my youth.

Fleeing, almost in tears now, I find another room, this one floor-to-ceiling taxidermy. The poor animals' dead glass eyes watch me from every direction and within them, I can see the figure. It's inside every case, every creature, every eyeball, over and over and over. Its hood's still up, but in every single reflection, it has one hand beating on the glass, like it's trapped in the animals themselves. It's terrifying and I can't bear it and I keep running and I *hate* myself—

Smack!

Not looking where I'm going, I run head first into the chest of a very tall man.

Startled, I jump back. He has thinning grey hair and a lean, kind face. There's a pair of round spectacles propped on his forehead. Forestalling any apology, he holds up a hand.

"What are you doing in here?" He sounds as surprised as I feel.

"Um." I've crashed back to reality with a bump, and it takes me a minute. "I got lost?"

"Your kind aren't allowed in here, you know that."

"My *kind?*" The words make no sense. The man doesn't look snobby. He looks affably scruffy, and I take a guess that he's the owner or manager. There's a line of silver hoops in one ear, and a tattoo on the back of one arm, a sun and moon that are half-and-half, and done in black. It's old enough to be blurring at the edges.

Seeing me look, he smiles. "Let me take you to the door," he says. He gestures with one spread hand, showing me away from the dead things.

I want to leave, of course I do, but something about this is bothering me. *My kind.* Does he know about it, the figure in the glass? Maybe – and the idea sideswipes me from nowhere – maybe he *put* it there?

The thought make me retreat further, eyeing the man warily from head to foot. He's wearing a lot of fraying cotton, most of it black, and his eyes are a gentle blue. Unbidden, I start thinking about storybook rituals, with symbols on the floor, and skulls, and candles, and people chanting from ancient tomes. There could be *any* kind of room, hidden here somewhere.

"I didn't meant to scare you," the man says, seeing my reluctance. The spread hand hasn't moved. "Let's you out of here shall we?"

I don't move. Glancing sideways, I look for the reflection.

I find it, in the glass front of the closest taxidermy case. The animal within is a bear, up on its hand paws, with patchy fur and a hideously contorted snarl. One of its ears is higher than the other. It's quite horrible, but it's not what I'm looking at. In front of it, one hand still pressed to the glass, is the hooded figure. It's stopped, the bear looming above it, and I swear it's still looking at me.

Looking at me, like it's trying tell me something.

The man glances, then sighs.

"And that's exactly why you shouldn't be in here." With a sharp dart, he grabs my arm, his fingers surprisingly strong. "Come on, let's get back where you belong."

Where you belong.

As he pulls me, the refection beats its fist on the glass. The gesture is urgent, but utterly silent. I try to pull away, needing to know what all this means, but the man's grip is like a vice.

"You should never have come in here," he says. His tone is getting bleaker by the moment. "Your type isn't welcome, you know that. You have to stay outside."

Outside.

For the first time, I realise something critical: I don't know what's out there. I don't know where I came from, or how I got here. I remember my childhood, but nothing else. Had I been shopping? Wandering the lanes and sideroads? What does the front of this store look like? What's its name?

What's *my* name?

The question brings a sudden sense of emptiness, a pit beneath my feet, and I panic. My stomach drops and I fight frantically, twisting and turning, tears streaking my face. In the reflection, the figure bangs the glass even harder. By the gestures, I think it's shouting.

Your type isn't welcome.

Who am I? Where did I come from? How did I get in here?

I struggle to think, but my mind is filled with the shop, with its junks and treasures. I strive to think through them, but they clutter my awareness. The man's dragging me, his fingers like bone, their sharp tips grinding into my skin.

"Wait!" I say to him. 'Wait!"

Terrified now, needing an explanation, I dig in my heels. He ignores me, dragging me onwards. We reach a cross-section, with passageways leading in four directions. One corner is all bookcases, another offers a curved-legged table, and a hand-crank Singer sewing machine. My grandmother had one just like it, and the junk looms over me again, filling my thoughts. The man glances one way, changes his mind and heads another. Looking in both directions, I see that the route he's rejected has a line of upright mirrors. Four of them, side-by-side and in various sizes.

Shaking my head to clear it, I try and focus. Whatever that reflection is, he's consciously keeping me away from it.

Or it away from *me*.

Okay, I think to myself, *that's enough*.

With my free hand, I grab a bookcase. It's laden, and heavy. My grip is slippery, as there's nothing to get a real purchase on, but I'm trying to clear my head. Clear it of all the *stuff*.

Where you belong.

Outside.

Your type isn't welcome.

Maybe the figure in the mirror is trying to help me. Trying to tell me something.

I grip harder, refusing to get go. The man give a short exhalation, releases my arm and then turns on me. He looks like he's about to make a fight of it. "The door's not far," he says, the words edged in ice. "Don't make this difficult."

But my anger's rising now. "What is this place?" I ask him. "What's outside? What's going on?"

"Outside is your… home," he says, the pause brief but alarming. "And you need to go back to it."

"Who's the figure in the reflection?"

"They don't matter," he says. "You left them behind a very long time ago. Now, let go of the bookcase, before I get angry."

"No." I flood with more questions. I want to know who I am, who the refection is, and what they're trying to tell me. I want to know how I got in here, and why I can't remember anything past my childhood. I want to know my *name*.

With a sharp twist, he grabs my free arm and twists it, hurting my shoulder and forcing me to bend sideways. I cry out, and lose my grip on the bookcase.

"You're making me hurt you," the man says. "Don't do that."

I struggle, spitting questions, but it's useless. The man's completely ignoring me, now, just frog-marching me, one arm up my back, down the last corridor, walls of glassless oil-paintings to either side. We turn a corner, and I see a line of dark curtains, presumably covering windows. There's a door at the centre, wooden, and completely smothered by posters and cards.

There's nothing that can show a reflection.

He forces me to the door, using his free hand to open it. At the shock, we both stumble back.

He doesn't let me go – he was expecting this – but I stagger into him, raising my arm to cover my face. All in a second, it comes back to me: this bleak, howling darkness. I remember it now, being out here. I remember being alone, and terrified, and utterly, utterly lost, far more so that I've been in the shop. I remember white-cold terror, cowering in stone, street corners, or in overflowing bins, while *they* came past, looking for stray souls. I remember hiding, not looking at them, because one sight of them is supposed to drive you insane, and take everything from your mind. I remember scurrying down the grey road like some stray leaf and seeing the lights of the shop window. It was like a lone dream in centre of the madness, and I looked for the door – this door – like a way out, at last.

Outside is your home. You need to go back to it.

It's not the figure in the reflection who's trapped.

You left them behind a very long time ago.

It's me. I'm the wrong side of the glass.

I don't know if the man's aware of my thoughts, my understanding, but he tightens his grip, twisting my arm until I cry out.

"I can't leave this open," he says, and there's real fear in his tone. "Go on, back out you go."

He tries to force me down the short step. There's a street outside, but it's all grey and black, like a shadow of something real. The roadway is cobbled and there's no sky, only lamps. Their light is sickly and ghost-pale. The wind cries, lorn, and colourless rubbish billows in dusty whirlwinds. From somewhere, I think I can hear crying.

That same, white-cold terror comes back to me and I grab the doorframe, planting myself where I am. It means he can't shut the door, and if he's not actually strong enough to force me out, then he'll have to retreat, and let both of us back in.

He swears, fighting me, but terror has lent me strength and I'm not moving.

"Tell me," I say to him, back over my shoulder. "Tell me, and I'll let you close the door."

"Tell you what?" His fear is tangibly rising. He leans forwards, craning to see both ways down the street, and I can feel his heart. He's looking for *them*, and I wonder what will happen if *they* get into the shop. It's why he doesn't want me here, in case I've brought *them* with me.

But that's not answering my questions.

"Who am I?" I ask. "Who's the figure in the reflection?"

The man swears, the sound sharp with dread. There's something at the street's end, something faintly silver. It moves softly, unbothered by the wind, though its form seems oddly nebulous. Fear rises in my throat like sickness.

"Close the door," I say. "Or you know what'll happen. You'll lose everything, the shop. And you'll lose your mind."

He ignores me, fighting desperately to force me outside. He twists my arm further, hurting, and I kick him, backwards and hard. I hit his knee and he lurches. His grip loosens just enough, and I wrench my arm free. The movement almost dislocates my shoulder, but I don't care. Still in the doorway, with the door still open, I turn and confront him.

"You want this door closed, you tell me what's going on."

"It'll take you too," he tells me.

"I don't think that matters," I say. It's another gamble, but I'm pretty secure in the guess that he has much more to lose than I do.

He lunges, trying to take me by surprise and push me down the step, but I duck and he misses. "Oh no, you don't. You want this door closed? You explain."

With my back to the grey street, I can't see the silver light, but I can hear it. It's the noise *they* all make, the thin, horrible keening that lets you know they're coming and gives you the chance to hide. Something in me always thought that it sounded like pain, or grief. Like horror, or regret. Like they, too, are some sort of tormented soul.

"It'll make us like them," the man says. He sounds like his mouth is full of ashes. "The horrors will know no end."

"I don't care. The way I see it, I must be dead already."

Unmoving, I face him down, the keening getting closer by the moment. It makes my skin crawl. Wind and rubbish blow through the door and he stares back at me, as if unable to believe we're doing this. Then, all in a rush, he starts to gabble.

"You're not dead," he says. "You just got stuck. It happens sometimes, gates open unexpectedly and people fall through them. There are even some places that are permanent gates, usually places with lots of memories."

"Like this store," I say. I wonder if I'd known, on some level, when I'd seen its light. Known it was a way out.

He's still talking. "But permanently open gates are dangerous, and if *they* get in here—"

"Then they could get out the other side?"

"We'd have to destroy the store."

The keening is getting loud now, and there's a second one, softer but also closing. The noise is horrific, like something scraping down glass or metal, like the saw of a badly played fiddle. A moment later, I hear a third.

"They know," he says. "They're *coming*."

Dropping his shoulder, he barges me with his full weight. I lose my balance, and tumble backwards down the step. The flowing silver light is barely a stone's throw away, and I leap back upwards, hitting the door just as he tries to slam it in my face. I still don't know who the figure in the reflection is, other than someone from my past. They're presumably trying to help me, get me back through the gate.

But one thing at a time.

The door is a wooden barrier, hard and cold and physical, caught between us. The silver light is in the corner of my eye, and I try not to look, though I'm aware of its eyelessness, its mouth stretched in a silent scream.

Sickening fear redoubles my efforts and I heave, almost sobbing with the effort. Without warning, the resistance stops and I hear the man fall, hitting the floor with a curse. The silver light is close now, a claw, reaching for me. Sickened, I leap from its path, right through the door, and I trip over the man's tumbled form, falling right beside him.

For a split second, we stare at each other, united in utter horror.

The door is still open, and the silver light creeps into the building. I'm aware of a skull, I think, sockets hollow and teeth bared. Forcing myself not to look at it, I look down at the threadbare carpet instead.

See the man's round glasses, fallen from his forehead and sitting right there.

See the figure within, his hand stretched out to me.

His hood is down and I can see him clearly, now. He doesn't quite mesh with my memories – he's too old – but I'd know my brother anywhere, his long hair like mine and the scar down his cheek where he'd fallen off his Chopper, that time. Dad had picked him up.

The recollection is warm, safe. I remember him, crying his eyes out, in our father's arms. Remember Dad comforting him. Remember Mum, dabbing at the cut, and telling him to be careful. Remember watching it all from my child's eyes, worried that my brother was hurt.

I reach out a hand, touch the glass myself. Hear the man shriek denial as the silver thing comes for him.

And then everything is gone.

"Been closed years," my brother says. "You used to love it, when we were nippers. You'd pretend that it was some timeless doorway, like a portal to other realms. You'd fall though it and get stuck, so I had to rescue you. Or the other way round."

The afternoon sun is bright, warming my shoulders. Before us, a wall of MDF has gone up round the old junkshop, a sprawling great place that's been derelict since we were kids. Notices tell people to keep out, and that the site is being redeveloped by Johns Construction Ltd, part of the Considerate Builders Scheme. Hard hats and hi-vis must be worn by all staff.

I glance at my brother, portly now, but the scar on his cheek still visible. "Maybe it was," I grin. "Just because you've lost your imagination."

"Kids' games," he says, with affectionate scorn. He gestures at the crane and at the concrete lorries, parked to one side. "Six months from now, this'll all be flats."

The idea makes me sad. My brother has already turned away, probably thinking sensible things about supermarkets, but I dawdle, peeking between the boards. The junkshop is all crumbled – it's cracked and collapsing, covered in graffiti tags and infested with weeds – but somehow, I still love it. Always have. And I still think it might've been a portal. That, if you pour enough powerful memories into somewhere, then it can become something else.

"Lyndsey!"

My brother's calling me, and we have stuff to do. It's Sunday and we've got a family gathering this afternoon. He's coming over to help me cook. Like him, I should probably be thinking about the supermarket.

But I pause, just for a moment, and wonder about portals.

Something Peculiar

from

Mark Morris

Confetti

"...with a sound like a final breath..."

"NO SECOND thoughts?" Sam says.

Zoe frowns. "About what?"

"Well... y'know... about the fact that Rob... lived here?"

And died here. The words hang unspoken between them. Zoe sighs. "Course not. We've talked about this."

"I *know*," Sam says. "But that was before we got the keys. Before this place became ours."

Zoe is silent for a moment. She looks around at the wide hallway, tilts her head to take in the high ceiling, the stairs stretching upwards. When she answers Sam's question, her voice is quieter, almost tender.

"Rob loved this house. And his parents loved it before him. It's always been a happy place. A happy family home. I think he'd be glad that it was us moving in here. I think he'd give us his blessing."

Sam pulls a face. "I'm not so sure about that."

"Why not?"

"Well, because of what happened. We betrayed him. Both of us."

She looks momentarily sad. "I know. But it was a mistake, wasn't it?"

"Oh, thanks."

"No, I mean... it was a one-off. *Would* have been a one-off, if Rob hadn't died. It was only because we'd drunk too much that first time. It didn't mean anything, it was just drunken lust. But after… well, it was deeper then, wasn't it? It was proper emotions that brought us together. Grief."

"I'd like to think it was more than just grief."

"Well, yeah, of course. But that was the start of it. Mutual misery." She laughs. "The perfect basis for any relationship."

Sam scowls, and Zoe rolls her eyes, then slaps his arm. "Oh, come on, lighten up. It was a joke. Don't spoil the first moments in our first house by sulking."

"Sorry." He makes an effort to smile, then wrinkles his nose. "Smells a bit musty, doesn't it?"

"It's bound to. It's been sealed up for a year."

"Fifteen months," Sam says.

That's how long it's been since Rob died. Such a lot has happened since.

"We just need to open the windows, air the place out. Fresh paint. Fresh carpets. We'll make this house ours."

"Exorcise the ghosts," Sam says.

Now it was Zoe's turn to wrinkle her nose.

"Rob doesn't need exorcising. If his ghost haunts this place, it'll be a friendly one. A welcoming one. Apart from his mum and dad, we were the two people he loved most in the world. His fiancé and his best friend. He'd be glad to see us together. And glad that it's us who'll be looking after this place for him."

"As long as he doesn't insist on a threesome."

"Sam! Don't be gross." Zoe gives him her disapproving face, then saunters off, bypassing the stairs on her left, pushing open the door at the end of the corridor that leads into the kitchen.

As soon as she's out of sight, the light pouring in through the picture window at the top of the stairs darkens, throwing the hallway into shadow. Pulse quickening, Sam's gaze leaps to the upper landing. He half-expects to see a figure standing there, blocking the light. But the sudden dimness is caused by the sun slipping behind a cloud, nothing more.

❖

When Sam enters the kitchen, he finds it empty, the back door ajar. Through the wide window above the sink, he sees Zoe standing almost at the end of the long back garden, beside the sprawlingly overgrown raised beds, in which Rob's mother grew all the family's vegetable needs – potatoes, carrots, beans, onions. Zoe is motionless, staring up at the old pear tree, nestled in the corner beyond the compost bin, where the wooden back fence meets the stone side wall. The tree is twisted and bent, and though it stands free, it gives the impression it is using the fence and wall to support its decrepit frame. Despite its withered appearance, it is festooned with white blossom, spring's new growth. Sam can't help thinking that Zoe looks as though she is communing with the tree. The thought unsettles him. To break the spell, he clumps out into the back garden, being deliberately loud.

"There you are," he calls with false cheerfulness, striding towards her.

When she turns, the look on her face causes a momentary chill to spike through him, chest to gut. The intensity of her expression makes him falter.

"What's the matter?"

In the pause before she speaks, he feels the chill expanding inside him. Then her eyes flicker.

"This is where it happened, isn't it?" she says.

He expels a long breath, nods. "This is where they found him, yeah."

For a moment, her expression threatens to crumple, then she regains control. Her voice, though, is suddenly small, almost wheedling. "Why did he do it, Sam? What possessed him?"

Sam shrugs. "I'm pretty sure he didn't do it on purpose. He was ridiculously drunk that night. He must've had no idea what he was doing." He pauses. "I still feel responsible."

She says what she always says: "It wasn't your fault."

"Yeah, but... I should have looked after him better. Made sure he was okay."

Zoe grips his arm, says it again, more fiercely. "It wasn't your fault."

For a few seconds they're silent. They stand looking at the tree. Then Sam says, "We could have it cut down. I mean... if it's always going to remind you..."

"It wasn't the tree's fault," says Zoe.

"No, but... anyway. It's something to think about."

"Hmm," she says. "We don't have to make a decision now, though, do we?"

"No," says Sam, taking her hand. "We've got all the time in the world."

"Please don't hate me for this, Rob," Zoe says, and applies the shield-like steamer pad to the wall of the master bedroom. She holds it there for a few seconds as the escaping steam hisses like a trapped snake, then slides it to the left as she attacks the steamed patch of wallpaper with a metal scraper.

The steamer has done its job efficiently, and the old floral-patterned paper is now wet and bubbling, and lifts off easily. This room, overlooking the back garden, was once Rob's parents' bedroom, and now it will be hers and Sam's. The wallpaper is faded, scuffed and horribly old-fashioned, and Zoe knows that if he could speak, Rob would give her his blessing to make the house her own. Even so, she can't help but feel guilty as strip after strip of soggy paper detaches itself from the wall and flops at her feet like sloughed skin.

An hour later, she's done almost an entire wall, and is feeling sweaty and grimy beneath her dungarees. She's on the topmost rung of a metal stepladder, tackling the last bit, arm aching as she holds the steamer pad against the highest part of the wall, when she hears the thumping.

It comes from the attic, directly above, separated from her by no more than a foot or so of plaster and wood. It shocks her so much she jerks back, almost falling off the ladder.

Somehow, she manages to both keep a grip on the steamer pad and maintain her balance. Like a giant iron, the plastic pad gushes a cloud of superhot steam at the ceiling, creating a hot fog above her head that drifts down, speckling her face like perspiration. With shuffling thumps still coming from the attic (Zoe has the confused idea that the heat from the steam has awakened something), she descends the ladder and unplugs the steamer from the wall. Immediately, with a sound like a final breath, the steam gouting from the pad dwindles and dies. In the sudden silence, Zoe stands, hands clenched, looking up at the ceiling, as if she expects it to burst open. The thumping and scurrying continue, frantic and haphazard.

Rats, she thinks. *We've got rats up there. Or squirrels.*

She doesn't relish the thought of tackling either, but she can't ignore them; it isn't in her nature. Sam is at work and won't be home for another four, five hours. Besides which, she refuses to be the helpless female, hiding behind her big, tough man. Telling herself that even if it *is* rats, they won't attack her, she folds up the stepladder and carries it out of the bedroom, on to the landing. Here, in the centre of the ceiling, is a square panel resting snugly on top of a wooden frame, the entrance into the attic. Positioning the stepladder beneath it, she ascends to the top step. Before lifting the panel, she takes her mobile from her pocket and activates the torch app. Then she takes a deep breath and lifts the panel up and to one side.

Pointing her torch ahead of her like a weapon, she straightens up, her head and shoulders rising through the square gap in the hallway ceiling. Her torch beam picks out something moving rapidly and frenetically, from right to left. The movement is accompanied by a soft, panicked clattering.

She cries out, and flinches violently enough to make the stepladder wobble beneath her. Thankfully, it doesn't tip over, and after a moment's confusion, she recognises the sound and movement for what it is: a pair of pigeons, who have clearly got in through a half-open skylight.

Disturbed by her entrance, they exit the same way, leaving behind spatters of bird shit and a few feathers, white in the torchlight, which gently sink to the floor. For a few seconds, Zoe remains where she is, breathing hard to calm her racing heart. Then she expels a grunt of laughter and levers herself up and into the attic. She's crossing to the skylight to close it when her foot hits something that skitters across the floor with a metallic clinking sound.

She shines her torch on the object. It's a set of metal handcuffs. Surprised, she bends down and picks them up. The cuffs are closed and there's no sign of a key. Zoe, though, is slim, almost dainty – her best friend Laura once described her as 'a little elf' – and her hands are small, childlike. Experimentally, she slides one of the cuff bracelets over her right hand, and finds that, although it's a squeeze, the loop slides over the widest part of her hand easily enough. When she tries to slide her hand back out, though, it isn't so easy. Have the cuffs tightened without her realising? She feels a moment of alarm, tugs harder – and her hand slides free. She grunts with relief, drops the cuffs into her dungaree pocket, then crosses to the skylight.

It's only after she's closed the skylight, exited the attic, lifted the wooden panel back into place, and descended the stepladder that she realises something odd. The pigeons had left some shit and feathers behind, but if the skylight has been open for the past fifteen months, shouldn't there have been a lot more mess? It's *possible* that the birds had only just discovered the open skylight, but is it probable? Zoe is not sure. Perhaps it was the warmth of the central heating that attracted them? Perhaps it was the smell of food? Neither of these explanations seem particularly satisfying, but they're more palatable than the alternative:

that someone, for whatever reason, has been in the attic and opened the skylight within the last day or two.

"Sam, what the hell? Are you okay?"

His reaction to her producing the handcuffs had not been what she was expecting. After screwing up the gooey wallpaper, stuffing it into binbags and dumping it in the waste bin outside, she'd been washing her hands at the sink when he'd entered the kitchen.

"Productive day?" he'd said, tossing his car keys on the kitchen table.

She'd dried her hands, then turned round. "Interesting day. Look what I found."

She'd put her hand in her dungaree pocket, then withdrew it with the handcuffs dangling from her index finger.

Waggling her eyebrows provocatively, she'd said, "Kinky or what?"

She'd expected Sam to laugh, but instead the colour had drained from his face and his eyes had widened in shock. Then he'd taken a small, stumbling step backwards, as though pushed. That was when she asked him if he was okay.

His gaze jerking from the handcuffs to her face, he tries to make light of his reaction. Forcing a laugh, he says, "Sorry, Zo, it's just… where did you find those things?"

"In the attic." She explains about the pigeons, then raises her hand, causing the cuffs to jangle softly. "But what is it about them that freaked you out? You look as though you've seen a ghost."

"I have in a way." He laughs again, unconvincingly. "Sorry. Massive over-reaction."

"Explain."

He takes a breath, then says, "Those things. Rob was wearing them on the night he… died."

"What?"

He looks apologetic. "Sorry. Bit of a bombshell. But yeah. He was wearing them on his stag night. It was a shock seeing them again. It just… brought it all back in a rush."

"Why was he wearing handcuffs? Do I even want to know?"

Sam sighs. "Bloke stuff. Sorry. It wasn't my idea, but Nathan booked him a strippergram. She turned up in the pub, dressed as a policewoman. Pretended to arrest him. Handcuffed him to a chair, then put the key in her… well, in her cleavage, and told him the only way he could free himself was if he got the key out with his teeth."

Zoe rolls her eyes. "My god."

"Yeah, I know. Pretty juvenile. But, y'know, we were pissed up and…"

"No doubt you all thought it was hilarious."

"Well… we did, yeah. Sorry. But the thing is, when he was found, he had marks on his wrist. You know, from where he'd tried to yank himself free of the chair. It looked a bit suss, I suppose. The police asked us about it, but I guess they were happy with what we told them, because they never mentioned it again."

She shakes her head and rolls her eyes. "But how did the handcuffs end up in the attic?"

"Dunno. I presumed Rob had given them back to the…"

"Stripper."

"Yeah."

"Well, clearly he didn't," she says. "He must have kept them. Unless these aren't the same ones?"

Sam shrugs. "They look the same, but… I dunno. I suppose all handcuffs look pretty much the same, don't they?"

Grimacing, she tosses the handcuffs on to the table. "Whether they're the same ones or not, it's a mystery how they ended up in the attic. And also why the skylight was open. You haven't been up there, have you?"

He shakes his head. "No."

Two days later, the wallpaper in the master bedroom has been stripped and the walls painted a deep turquoise, which Zoe finds both dramatic and restful. She's done most of the work – she's on a two-week break from her marketing job – but Sam's mucked in during the evening, and yesterday he worked until after 11pm, while she crashed out with a bottle of Pinot Grigio and the latest series of *Bridgerton*.

Now, the paint has dried, and smells fresh and new rather than headache-inducingly pungent. The curtains from her old flat (they'll do the job until they can find something better) are up, and Zoe is eager to make a proper start on sorting out their clothes, which are still mostly packed in suitcases, or draped over furniture in the spare bedroom.

Sam owns eight suits (Rob only owned the one he'd bought for their wedding, and which he ended up being cremated in), seven of which are encased in nylon garment bags, and laid carefully over a wooden dining chair. Wrapping her arms around them, Zoe carries them into the bedroom and lays them on the floor. Tonight she and Sam will install the rest of their furniture in here, including their new bed, which is currently in a big flatpack box in the garage, and will no doubt prove far more difficult to put together than the 'Easy to Assemble' instructions claim.

She by no means believes in traditional gender roles, but she'll let Sam take the lead on that particular task. What he lacks in artistic appreciation he makes up for in practical skills, unlike Rob, who was almost the complete opposite. It's an idle thought, but it's one that catches her unawares. Suddenly she finds a wave of sadness, regret, longing, and yes, even guilt, washing over her.

Not for the first time, she wonders how different her life would have been if Rob hadn't died. She loves Sam (although not, she sometimes thinks guiltily, quite as much as he loves her), but she can't deny that he's not quite the soul mate that Rob would have been.

It's a cliché, but she and Rob were two halves of the same coin. *Sympatico.* So utterly devoted to one another that... *no.*

She frowns. She won't go there. She doesn't *deserve* to go there. How can she claim she was devoted to Rob when she let him down so badly? When she did the dirty on him by sleeping with his best friend three months before they were due to get married?

She's tried to justify it since – has told herself it meant nothing at the time; she was horribly drunk; it was a last, desperate fling, brought on by anxiety at the prospect of making the ultimate commitment. But whatever slant she puts on it, she can't quite convince herself. For her to have done that to Rob, there must have been *something* wrong between them, mustn't there? Their relationship can't have been *quite* as perfect as it's seemed since his death.

"Doesn't matter now," she says to herself, her voice rough. "Water under the bridge."

It *does* matter, though, and a thought she's had before, one that slides in at vulnerable moments, when she least expects it, suddenly pierces her heart like a slim, sharp blade.

That thought is: *did Rob know?* Did he somehow find out about her and Sam, and did that have a bearing, whether directly or indirectly, on his death? Sam swears he never breathed a word to anyone about what happened, and Zoe has certainly said nothing – even now that she and Sam are together, she feels deeply ashamed of her actions that night – and yet she can't help wondering whether Rob somehow *knew* nonetheless.

Don't go there.

The inner voice that speaks these words is full of anger, and she knows it's right – but even so. As she always does when her thoughts go down this route, she forces herself to look at the facts. And the facts are that Rob arrived home after his stag night spectacularly drunk, stripped off his clothes, and then, instead of crashing into bed, went back downstairs, stark naked, and outside into the back garden. And once there, he sat with his back against the old pear tree, and either passed out or fell asleep.

And was spotted by his next-door neighbour the following morning, dead and blue from exposure.

Misadventure. That had been the verdict of the inquiry. No one could ever truly know why Rob had decided to sit out in the freezing cold garden instead of collapsing into bed, but the general consensus was that he must have felt sick, and so decided, in his drunken stupor, that it would be a good idea to get a breath of fresh air before going to sleep.

"Oh, Rob," she sighs, and speaking his name suddenly makes her feel as if he's *there*, in the room. She feels a cold tickle on the back of her neck, a shiver between her shoulder blades. She turns quickly... but of course, the room is empty, and the open door shows her there's no one standing on the landing.

She laughs shakily, then turns back to the task in hand. Bending forward, she unzips the first of the nylon garment bags and lifts out the suit within. It's Sam's bright blue three-piece, wool with silk lining, that he wore on their wedding day. As she holds it up, confetti drifts down from it, swirling in the sudden breeze that comes in through the open window.

She has a sudden impression – something she glimpses from the corner of her eye – that the fall of confetti is somehow replicated, or echoed, in the garden. She glances towards the window, and sees white flakes falling from the pear tree, speckling the lawn.

It's blossom, of course, not confetti. The upward sprawl of branches is currently smothered in it. But then something else catches her eye, and her body gives a lurch of shock. Halfway up the tree, partly concealed by branches and blossom... isn't that a figure crouched there? She steps towards the window. It's a bit too far away, and therefore hard to make out, but she can't shake the impression there's a man perched on a branch, bent knees touching his chin, arms wrapped around his shins.

She drops Sam's wedding suit to the floor and shakily takes out her phone. Feeling exposed, as if the dark figure in the tree is watching her every move, she clicks on the camera app, then raises the phone until the pear tree is dead centre of her screen. Using the thumb and index finger of her free hand, she expands the picture, zooming in on the dark shape. The hand which is holding the phone is shaking, and for a split-second the picture goes out of focus. Then it steadies, sharpens… and there's nothing there. No figure in the tree. No dark patch within the branches.

Shadows, she thinks. An optical illusion.

On the floor at her feet, flecks of confetti, little hearts and horseshoes, stir in the breeze.

Zoe is in two minds about The Wise Owl. It's their closest pub, and therefore their new local, but it's also a place where she and Rob spent many happy hours together, and the last time she set foot through the door, maybe eighteen months ago, she was *with* Rob, as his fiancé.

She knows she can't avoid it forever, though, and so when Sam suggests grabbing a bite to eat there before tackling the job of putting their new bed together, she reluctantly agrees.

She braces herself for either disapproval or sympathy, but in the event, she's subjected to neither. If anyone *does* recognise her, they don't let on. The bar staff all seem to have changed from when she was last here, and the landlord, who always said hello to Rob but barely ever acknowledged her, appears not to recognise her.

That doesn't stop her from feeling tense all the way through their meal, though, which Sam, to her annoyance, seems to find amusing.

"Why does it bother you?" he asks.

"It just does, that's all."

"But why?"

"I don't want people to think badly of me."

"Why should they think badly of you?"

She glares at him. "Are you *completely* insensitive, Sam? Because barely a year after my fiancé dies, not only am I shacking up with his best man, but I'm moving into his old house. How do you think that looks?"

Sam shrugs, but he's sulky now. "Who cares what these people think? And by the way, we're not shacking up, we're married. And I'm *not* insensitive."

Zoe wants to tell him to wind his bottom lip in, but she bites back the words. They've got a lot to do tonight, and she doesn't want an atmosphere. Instead she says, "All right, I'm sorry. But surely you can see why I'm feeling tense?"

He shrugs again. "Suppose."

She clenches her teeth, then forces a smile. "Shall we go?"

As soon as Sam opens the front door of their house, Zoe knows something is wrong. There's a breeze blowing through the downstairs corridor, which there shouldn't be. Her first thought is that she left the bedroom window open, and the wind has picked up. But almost immediately she realises the breeze is not coming from upstairs. It's blowing directly at them from the direction of the kitchen.

The kitchen door creaks, and opens a little wider as the wind pushes against it. Even before Sam can switch on the hall light, Zoe is striding towards the back of the house, wondering whether she's about to face an intruder. Shoving open the door hard enough to slam into anybody who might be crouched behind it, she steps over the threshold, reaches to her right and slaps at the light switch. The door bangs back against the wall at the same instant that the room is flooded with light. Zoe sees with a glance that the room is empty, but alarm still surges through her body like nausea.

The back door into the garden is wide open.

She doesn't realise Sam is standing at her shoulder until he mutters, "Fuck." She's about to move towards the open door when he grabs her arm hard enough to hurt.

"Let me go first," he says, but instead of moving directly to the door, he takes a couple of sideways steps and grabs the biggest carving knife from the knife block on the counter.

"Seriously?" Zoe says, scathingly enough that he flashes her a wounded look.

"There might be burglars out there," he says.

"Yeah, and if you use that on them, you'll be the one in court."

"I'm not going to use it," he says irritably. "This is just to scare them with."

"Hmm," she says, but he's stumping to the door now, clearly offended by her reaction. Deciding it's best not to get him any more worked up, she follows him into the garden.

As soon as they step outside, the motion sensor light comes on, throwing harsh white light across the long back lawn. Both of them do a double take at what it reveals.

"What the fuck?" Sam mutters.

There are clothes strewn all around the garden, filthy, crumpled, and torn. At first Zoe assumes it's a random act of destruction, but then Sam wails, "Fuck's sake! My suits!"

And suddenly she realises he's right. The only clothes here are Sam's suits, all of which she hung in the wardrobe earlier. If his suits had been the only things in there, she'd assume the invader(s) had just grabbed the first things they could find, and trashed them. But no, she'd spent most of the afternoon transferring their clothes from the spare room to the master bedroom, and so alongside Sam's suits were plenty of her own clothes – dresses, skirts, jackets.

"Why would someone *do* this?" Sam whines. And then a weird look crosses his face, as if he's realised something. The expression causes gooseflesh to ripple down Zoe's arms, which is nothing to do with the chilly spring breeze.

"What?" she says. "What are you thinking?"

He looks at her, blinks. Then says, "We should check the house. Make sure there's no one upstairs. See if anything's missing."

He pushes past her and stomps back into the house, holding the knife down by his side.

Telling herself it must have occurred to him that the intruders might still be here, yet feeling in her gut that the expression on his face was due to something else entirely, she gives his ravaged suits a final glance, then follows him.

It's only later, after the police have gone, that Sam starts to shake. While they were here, he was indignant, righteously angry at this violation of his and Zoe's privacy, but as soon as they leave, promising vaguely that they'll look into it, he all but falls onto the settee and begins to shiver so hard his teeth chatter like castanets.

"Hey," Zoe says, sitting beside him and wrapping her arms around him, "come on, it's okay."

He laughs harshly. "Okay? Are you kidding? How is any of this okay?"

She thinks he's overreacting, but she says, "I know it's a pisser about the suits, but it could have been worse. They could have trashed the whole house. They could have robbed us blind. But like the police said, the fact that they didn't probably means it was just kids, out to cause trouble."

In truth, she finds it odd that they *weren't* robbed blind. As far as they've been able to tell, nothing is missing, and only Sam's suits have been damaged. That suggests to her a personal attack. But who is mad enough, or angry enough, to do this to Sam? An old girlfriend? A work colleague? When the police asked him earlier, he insisted he couldn't think of anyone, vehemently denied he had any enemies.

Too vehemently? Again, Zoe gets the feeling he's keeping something from her. But maybe she's just being paranoid.

"I'll put the kettle on," she says, "make us a cup of tea."

"Yeah, cos that'll make everything better," he says scathingly.

She scowls. "All right then. I *won't* make you a cup of tea. But I fucking want one."

She stands up abruptly. Before she can move away, his hand clamps around her wrist.

"Ow! That hurts!"

For a second he looks irritated – then his face changes, becomes contrite.

"Sorry," he says, releasing her. "I'm just wound up, that's all."

Yeah, well, don't take it out on me. Instead of snapping the words that leap into her mind, she says, "I'm making you a cup of tea, whether you want one or not. You need to calm down, Sam."

Before he can respond, she stalks out of the room and into the kitchen. She fills the kettle and turns it on, then glances at the now-closed back door.

Another weird thing. The door wasn't forced, it was just open, which means one of them must have left it unlocked when they went out. But she could have sworn it was locked, because neither of them has been in the back garden today, and she's always assiduous about checking the locks every night before going to bed. But hey. It's not an unsolvable mystery; she must have been mistaken, that's all. Maybe one of them dumped something in the bin outside and forgot to lock the door when they came back in. It happens.

While she's waiting for the kettle to boil, the motion sensor light in the garden comes on again. Her eyes flicker towards the window over the sink, but she's not unduly alarmed. The light does that sometimes, especially if it's windy, as it is now. The light illuminates the strewn and crumpled jackets and trousers, which they'd left out there so the police could see what had been done. She decides to go and collect them while she's waiting for the kettle to boil. Maybe some of them will be salvageable.

Opening the back door, she enters the garden and begins scooping up the items of clothing, shaking each one free of dirt and debris before draping it over her arm. She goes about the task methodically, starting with the item closest to the back door. The last few things are at the far end of the garden, outside the range of the light, close to the back fence and the old pear tree. As she picks up the penultimate item, which is nothing but a crumpled mound on the lawn, she hears the branches of the pear tree creaking in the brisk spring breeze.

She pauses, curious and a little unsettled. As well as the creaking of the branches, she can hear a metallic jangling. She thinks of ghosts clanking chains, and then of potential attackers wielding them as weapons, but the jangling is lighter than that. It fades for a moment, and then, when another strong breeze sweeps through the garden, she hears it again, and this time she can tell it's coming from the direction of the tree. She peers into the darkness. Can she see something glinting on one of the lower branches? She moves closer – and then sees what it is.

It's the handcuffs. The ones she found in the attic. They're attached to one of the pear tree's lower branches, swinging back and forth in the breeze.

They don't have time to build their new bed, and so it's another uncomfortable night on the blow-up. Zoe is drifting off to sleep, her back to Sam, when he turns over, creating a displacement of air, causing her body to lurch into wakefulness.

"Zo," he hisses, "are you awake?"

She sighs. "I am now."

"Sorry," he says. "I just wanted you to know… I really love you."

"Thanks," she says, hoping he's not feeling amorous. She just wants to sleep.

"No," he says. "I mean it. I *really* love you. I love you so much. I've loved you ever since I've known you. I've never really told you before, but even when you and Rob were together, I was crazy about you."

She's fully awake now. His intensity is such that she doesn't know how to respond. "Bit inappropriate," she says eventually, trying to make light of it, "but… okay."

"I just…" She gets the impression he's struggling to express himself, perhaps even a little choked with emotion. "I just wanted you to know, that's all. It's important that you know how much."

Should she turn to face him? If she does, the blow-up will ripple like a sound wave, and besides, she's so exhausted after the night they've just had she doesn't want to move. So, instead she says, "Thanks, Sam. I appreciate it. And I love you too."

She feels the warm weight of his hand on her hip. It makes her feel vaguely unsettled, to the extent she wants to ask him to remove it, but she doesn't want to hurt his feelings. So she says nothing, and instead concentrates on breathing deeply and steadily, a relaxation technique she employed after Rob's death whenever she felt her grief threatening to escalate into panic. The technique works, and eventually she gets so used to his hand that she can't feel it anymore, and she falls asleep.

She wakes to the sound of hacking.

It's a meaty, visceral sound. It immediately evokes intonations of violence, of anger. Zoe jolts upright, her heart pumping hard.

Her sleep-fuddled mind struggles to bring the sound into context. Where is it coming from? It sounds distant, but not *too* distant.

She turns to wake Sam, but his side of the bed is empty. Funny that she didn't feel him get up, considering how much the blow-up ripples when he moves. Either he exited super-carefully, so as not to wake her, or she was in a profoundly deep sleep.

Grabbing her phone from the floor beside the bed, she sees it's 7:12am, which is still nearly twenty minutes short of when their alarm goes off. Rolling off the bed and stumbling upright, she pushes hair off her forehead, then tries to massage some life into her face. A little more alert now, she works out that the hacking sound, which is steady, relentless, is coming from the back of the house.

The blow-up bed is downstairs, in the front room (they prop it in the hall during the day), so she makes her way along the hallway towards the kitchen. It's chilly this morning, and even with her bed socks on, the stone tiles are cold beneath her feet. As she pushes the kitchen door open, the hacking sound grows louder. She crosses to the window above the sink and looks out, and her gaze is immediately drawn to a blur of movement at the end of the garden.

Blinking, focusing, she sees that it's Sam. He's wielding an axe, and he's frenziedly attacking the ancient pear tree by the back fence, trying to chop through its thick, gnarled trunk.

She feels indignant, even horrified. Although she's only wearing a thin T-shirt, shorts and socks, she rushes across to the back door, then out into the garden. Running down the length of the dew-damp lawn, she shouts angrily, "What the fuck, Sam? What are you *doing?*"

When he swings round, she is momentarily alarmed. He looks *wild*, his face red and sweaty, eyes glaring, mouth hanging open as he pants. For a moment he seems not to recognise her, and she is suddenly afraid he is about to run at *her*, swinging the axe.

But then his face changes. And suddenly he looks no longer angry, but confused, ashamed. He looks like a small boy who has been caught doing something he shouldn't. His eyes flicker to the axe in his hand, as if it should somehow take responsibility for what he's doing.

And although he doesn't let go of the axe, his arm suddenly drops, as if it's become very heavy.

"I was just…" he stammers, before falling silent.

"Just what?"

He grimaces, glances at the tree, into whose trunk he's hacked a mangled wound.

"We said we were going to cut it down, didn't we? We *said*."

It's like he's pleading with her, desperate for her vindication. She shakes her head.

"We mentioned it, but we hadn't decided anything. But that's not the point, Sam." She gestures at the tree, the axe, his wildness. "Why now? And why like this? I mean, what even *is* this? It's seven in the morning, for God's sake."

He looks flustered, but also evasive. "I thought I'd make a start. I have to go to work soon."

"That's not an answer. This… this is madness, Sam. What's happened?"

Now he looks defensive, fearful. His face is a kaleidoscope of emotions, flickering wildly from one to the next. "What do you mean?"

"I mean, why do you wake up at the crack of dawn and suddenly decide you need to attack the tree? Something must have made you do it."

"I don't know. I feel…"

"Feel what?"

"It doesn't like us being here."

"What doesn't? The tree?"

"The… the tree. The house. Everything it represents."

She goes still. Frowns. Quietly she says, "Are you talking about Rob? Are you saying Rob doesn't want us here? Is that what you honestly think? Because of what happened last night?"

"Not just last night."

"What then?"

Now he looks evasive again. "I don't want to talk about it."

"*Why* don't you want to talk about it? What aren't you telling me?"

"*Nothing.*" It's a child's whine. A child's denial.

"There must be – *Sam, look out!*"

It all happens in a split-second. Alerted by movement above Sam's head, she looks up, and sees what at first looks like an upper branch of the tree reaching down towards him. For a confused second, she thinks the tree has come alive, and is lowering a claw-like hand to scoop him up.

Then she realises what's really happening. The tree is old, and no doubt partly rotten. And Sam's attack upon it has sent shuddering impact after shuddering impact up through the old wood, causing it to split, to crack, to tear away.

The upper branch that detaches itself from the tree is longer than Sam is tall, and doubtless several times as heavy. As she screams, her eyes fixed on the falling branch, he looks up too, and she sees horror transform his face into a trio of widening dark circles. The branch crashes through smaller branches as it descends, causing blossom to explode outwards, engulfing Sam like a blizzard, or a shower of confetti. For a moment, all she sees is the branch and the blossom, and then the branch crashes to the ground, bits of it flying off in all directions, creating a cloud of dust and debris.

"*Sam!*" she screams. "*Sam! Sam!*" Such is her panic that she feels as though she's tearing her throat; she tastes blood at the back of it.

She rushes forward, terrified of what she might see – and then she hears coughing, panting. She sees a dark shape on the ground. Sees Sam, fingers digging into the lawn, dragging himself through the mud and the grass like a soldier crawling across a battlefield.

She hurls herself towards him, drops to her knees, her hands all over his back, his arms, his head, looking for injuries. The echoes of the branch hitting the ground still seem to reverberate in her mind.

"Are you okay? Are you hurt?"

He twists his head, looks up at her, eyes wide with trauma but not with pain.

"No, I'm fine," he gasps. "He didn't get me."

It's not until much later, when Zoe is lying in the bath, trying to relax, that Sam's words come back to her: *He didn't get me.*

He? Is that really what he said? Surely she must have misheard? Isn't it more likely he said, '*It* didn't get me'? Meaning the tree branch?

She tries to cast her mind back, but whenever she pictures Sam's face, whenever she hears his voice, she sees and hears the same thing: *He didn't get me.*

Not *it.*

He.

She lies back, closes her eyes. The water is luxuriously warm. For the first time today she feels calm, able to think. After Sam's near-fatal accident that morning, he had been a wreck – at first weepy and jittery, and then angry and defiant, but also irrational, evasive.

As soon as they re-entered the house, he made for the drinks cupboard, poured himself a generous measure of whisky and gulped it down, and then another.

"Hey, slow down," she said. "It's 7.30 in the morning. You've got to go to work, remember."

He goggled at her. "Work? After what just happened? I'm not going to work." And defiantly he poured himself a third whisky.

"Why not?" she said. "You're okay, aren't you? You're not injured? Just give yourself—"

He'd cut her off with an almost hysterical shriek of laughter.

"Zo," he had cried in disbelief, "are you mad? Do you honestly think I would leave you with that…"

He wafted a hand vaguely.

"With what? That evil tree out there?"

He glared at her, gulped at his drink. "It's not the tree."

"What is it then?"

He had looked away from her then, and the expression on his face had been impossible to decipher. Was he confused? Distressed? Traumatised? There were elements of all those things in his eyes, in the way his mouth worked. But he had also looked… trapped. Like an animal hounded into a corner.

"This was a mistake," he mumbled.

She blinked. "What was? Do you mean us?"

This time his eyes had opened wide not in fear, but in astonishment. "No! Not us! *Of course* not us! How could you even suggest that? We're the only thing in this… *clusterfuck* that makes sense. I'm talking about *this*. This house. Coming here. What were we thinking?"

Before she could process this, he shot out a hand and grabbed a fistful of her T-shirt.

"Let's leave," he said eagerly. "Let's just pack up and go. We'll put the house back on the market. Find somewhere else to live."

Wrenching herself free, she said angrily, "Are you mad? Listen to yourself, Sam! We're not moving. We can't afford to, for one thing. And for another, I can't take any more upheaval. Not now. You just need to… calm down. Put things in perspective."

He laughed then, high and wild. "Perspective? There *is* no fucking perspective. Can't you see that?"

"No, I can't. Look, just… go for a walk. Or lie down for a bit. Try and get your head together."

Instead of following her advice, he had poured himself a fourth whisky. Then a fifth. A sixth. By mid-morning he was hammered. Rambling, dissembling, occasionally weeping. By mid-afternoon he was passed out on the blow-up in the front room, and that was where he had been ever since.

And now it was evening. Coming up to 8pm. Dark outside. Sam has been asleep for the past five hours. Zoe is hoping he'll sleep through until morning. Wake up tomorrow in a calmer, more rational frame of mind.

She sighs, allowing her mind to drift, to free associate. Those words of Sam's still won't leave her. *He didn't get me.* Who is '*he*'? There is only one possible answer as far as she can see.

He must have meant Rob. But that's crazy. Does Sam honestly think everything that's happened – the ruined suits, the tree branch – have been caused by her ex-fiancé's… what? Vengeful spirit?

If so, he's losing his grip on reality; he needs psychological help. Apart from anything else, his reasoning doesn't make sense. Even if there were such things as ghosts, why would he think Rob, of all people, would be out to get him? Because Sam has stepped into his shoes? Taken his house, his girl, his unlived life?

But Rob wasn't like that. He was the sweetest man. Kind. Understanding. Forgiving. He wasn't vindictive. And it wasn't Sam's fault that Rob died.

Was it?

Her mind churns, tries to make sense of all that's happened this past week, to make odd-shaped pieces fit into a picture she can't yet see. Why was Sam *quite* so shocked when she produced the handcuffs? Why, after asking who would do such a thing to his suits, did that weird look cross his face, as if he had just realised something? Why, in bed last night, did he tell her he loved her with such intensity, such desperation? It was as if… as if he was terrified she would find out something about him that would make her love him less. And why did he lose it this morning, and attack the tree, the place where Rob had died, with such ferocity? Such vehemence?

She thinks again about the handcuffs. Why had she found them dangling from the tree last night? Who had put them there? Sam? The intruder?

All these things – the handcuffs, the suits, the tree – could be explained away if it wasn't for… for Sam's reaction.

This, she realises, is truly what's unsettling her. Not the events themselves, but how he has responded to them.

The fear. The anger. The paranoia. But, more than that… the *guilt*.

Yes. That's it. When she produced the handcuffs. When he saw his ruined suits scattered about the garden. When he told her he loved her. Even after his near-fatal accident with the tree. His overriding reaction, manifesting as rage, as desperation, as fear, even as love, had been *guilt*.

And more specifically, the guilt that comes with the fear of being discovered.

"What did you do?" she whispers. And as the words leave her lips, she suddenly feels she is no longer alone in the bathroom. She has had her eyes closed all this time, has been lying back in the warm water, her thoughts drifting along with her body. But now, sensing a presence, she sits up, displacing water so suddenly that it surges in a wave and slops over the side of the bath, slapping the wooden floor.

A split-second before she opens her eyes, she feels light kisses on her skin, raining down on her face and shoulders. Then her eyes open, gritty with warmth, and she sees swirls of white in front of her.

Confetti.

No, not confetti. Blossom. It's blossom. Tiny white petals of pear blossom. Dozens of them. They drift down, as if from nowhere, sticking to her wet skin, settling in her hair, speckling the bath water.

The door to the bathroom is behind her, over her left shoulder. When it creaks, she spins, displacing more water, which hits the floor in a series of splats. And she sees that the door, which was closed, is now very slightly ajar. And she also sees… no, glimpses… no, gets an impression of… a dark shape, moving away, along the landing.

"Sam?" she calls. A pear blossom petal drifts down, sticks to her lower lip; she swipes it away, absent-mindedly. "Sam? Is that you?"

No answer. And no sound of movement from beyond the door. No creak of weight on the floorboards or stairs.

Heart thudding, she stands up, reaches for her towel, which is on a wooden chair with a wicker seat, next to the bath. She shakes blossom from the towel and wraps it around herself. She is shivering, not so much with cold but reaction.

What the fuck? What the *fuck?* What is happening here? Still wrapped in the towel, she pads across to the door, pulls it all the way open.

The house is quiet. Silent. But all the way along the landing, like breadcrumbs leading a child through a dark forest in a fairy tale, is a trail of white pear blossom petals.

"Sam?" she calls again. And then, receiving no answer, she calls out another name.

"Rob?"

The fact that she half-expects a response makes her heart drum even harder. But there *is* no response. Of course there isn't. Even so, that sense of… of expectation, of *possibility*, won't go away.

Standing on the landing, water running down her legs, pooling around her feet, she rubs vigorously at her hair, her skin, drying herself. She does it quickly, almost frantically, feeling there's little time to waste, without quite knowing why.

Still damp, she ducks back into the bathroom, grabs her clothes from where she dumped them on top of the washing basket, dresses quickly. Wet hair caressing the back of her neck like a cold hand, she laces her trainers with trembling fingers, then exits the bathroom.

She half-expects the trail of petals to have disappeared, but no, they're still there. They trail down the stairs. She crushes them underfoot as she descends.

She thinks again of the handcuffs dangling from the tree, and she thinks of Rob being found there, dead from exposure. *Was* he alone that night, too drunk to know what he was doing? Or was he led outside, handcuffed to the tree, and simply left there for hours, unable to get away?

I really love you. I love you so much. I've loved you ever since I've known you... I just wanted you to know, that's all. It's important that you know how much.

She reaches the bottom of the stairs. The petals trail all the way along the ground floor landing, and through the half-open kitchen door, whereupon they're swallowed by darkness.

The kitchen door moves an inch or two, pushed by a breeze, which she feels sweep across her, chilling her still-damp skin. She remembers last night, coming home, the same thing happening, finding the back door open.

"Sam!" she shouts, alarmed. She runs to the living room door, which, like the kitchen door, is ajar. She shoves it open. "Sam!"

He's not there; he's not on the blow-up where she left him. His clothes are, though. Strewn about, as though removed in a hurry. And liberally speckled, like the bed, like the floor, in small white petals.

Alarm escalating into panic, she exits the living room and runs down the corridor. Reaching the kitchen door, she slams it open with the flats of her hands and bursts through.

She doesn't even stop to turn on the kitchen light. Instead, she heads straight for the open back door. The garden is mostly dark, though a little light bleeds through from surrounding houses and streetlights, enough for her to see white petals leading all the way up the long lawn to the back fence.

To the pear tree.

She follows the petals, running, panting. The movement sensor light comes on, but it doesn't reach as far as the tree, which sprawls into the sky like a frozen eruption.

And at its base... a large white shape.

It takes another few steps before the white shape, vague in the darkness, becomes discernible as a figure. A man.

Naked. Lying sprawled against the trunk of the tree, legs splayed before him, left arm upraised.

Closer, and she recognises Sam. Sees his arm is upraised because it's handcuffed to a lower branch. Hand hanging limply.

Zoe wonders if he struggled. Wonders if he called out her name in fear. If he even had chance to do so.

He can neither struggle nor call out now, because he's dead. That much is obvious. His bulging eyes are glazed in terror. His face is black and bloated.

His mouth yawns open, because it is stuffed, *crammed*, with pear blossom petals. They have spilled from his bottom lip and adhered to his saliva-slick chin. They have stuck to the tears on his cheeks like macabre facial adornments.

Even now, in the darkness, blossom drifts lazily down from the upper branches of the tree, forming languid spirals in the air.

It settles on Sam's corpse, and on the ground all around him.

Like confetti.

Guy Adams
guyadams.info

Holly Blades
instagram.com/lifeofholly

Sarah Brooks
linktr.ee/sarahbrookswriting

Emma J Gibbon
emmajgibbon.com

Timothy J Jarvis
timothyjjarvis.wordpress.com

John Langan
johnpaullangan.wordpress.com

Tim Major
timjmajor.com

Alexander Milner
alexmilner.co.uk

Mark Morris
markmorrisfiction.com

Danie Ware
danacea.ghost.io

Marian Womack
marianwomack.com

blackshuckbooks.co.uk

Also available:

GREAT BRITISH HORROR 1:
GREEN AND PLEASANT LAND

FEATURING STORIES BY

JASPER BARK
A.K. BENEDICT
RAY CLULEY
JAMES EVERINGTON
RICH HAWKINS
V.H. LESLIE
LAURA MAURO
ADAM MILLARD
DAVID MOODY
SIMON KURT UNSWORTH
BARBIE WILDE

GREAT BRITISH HORROR 2:
DARK SATANIC MILLS

FEATURING STORIES BY

CHARLOTTE BOND
PAUL FINCH
ANDREW FREUDENBERG
GARY FRY
CATE GARDNER
CAROLE JOHNSTONE
PENNY JONES
GARY MCMAHON
MARIE O'REGAN
JOHN LLEWELLYN PROBERT
ANGELA SLATTER

Also available:

GREAT BRITISH HORROR 3:
FOR THOSE IN PERIL

FEATURING STORIES BY

STEPHEN BACON

SIMON BESTWICK

GEORGINA BRUCE

KAYLEIGH MARIE EDWARDS

JOHNNY MAINS

PAUL MELOY

THANA NIVEAU

ROSALIE PARKER

KIT POWER

GUY N. SMITH

DAMIEN ANGELICA WALTERS

GREAT BRITISH HORROR 4:
DARK AND STORMY NIGHTS

FEATURING STORIES BY

G.V. ANDERSON

SIMON AVERY

M.R. CAREY

PAUL M. FEENEY

KATH DEAKIN & TIM LEBBON

ALISON LITTLEWOOD

MAURA MCHUGH

PRIYA SHARMA

PHIL SLOMAN

CATRIONA WARD

REN WAROM

Also available:

Also available:

GREAT BRITISH HORROR 7:
MAJOR ARCANA

FEATURING STORIES BY

GARY BUDDEN
DAN COXON
MALCOLM DEVLIN
STEVEN J DINES
CARLY HOLMES
IDA KEOGH
ALISON MOORE
LYNDA E RUCKER
JONATHAN SIMS
ANNA TABORSKA
CONRAD WILLIAMS

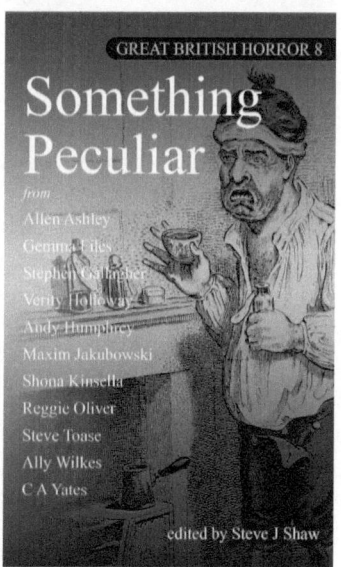

GREAT BRITISH HORROR 8:
SOMETHING PECULIAR

FEATURING STORIES BY

ALLEN ASHLEY
GEMMA FILES
STEPHEN GALLAGHER
VERITY HOLLOWAY
ANDY HUMPHREY
MAXIM JAKUBOWSKI
SHONA KINSELLA
REGGIE OLIVER
STEVE TOASE
ALLY WILKES
C A YATES

Also available:

GREAT BRITISH HORROR 9:
SOMETHING PECULIAR

FEATURING STORIES BY

TIFFANI ANGUS
LENA BEASLEY-SILVERWOOD
JAMES BROGDEN
JAN EDWARDS
GRADY HENDRIX
PAUL KANE
JONATHAN OLIVER
ROSANNE RABINOWITZ
NICHOLAS ROYLE
MICHAEL MARSHALL SMITH
ASHLEY STOKES